He wanted just ☐ with Eve…

There was so much to say, and yet Noah didn't have the words to say it.

There was something about Eve that tugged at him, that hinted at more just beneath the surface, and even though he knew that whatever friendship they formed would be cut off the minute she left Redemption, he couldn't bring himself to stop yet.

"What do you need?" he asked softly.

"I don't know…" Eve's eyes sparkled with unshed tears. "I think I need a friend."

"You have that," he said earnestly. "If I count at all…"

"We are very unlikely friends," she whispered.

He reached up and moved a tendril of stray hair off her forehead.

"I didn't expect to feel what I do when I'm with you—" He swallowed the words. He didn't know how to name what he felt.

What was it about this woman that drew him in this way? She was the mother of the child his brother hoped to adopt.

Noah wasn't supposed to complicate her life…

Patricia Johns writes from Alberta, Canada. She has her Hon. BA in English literature and currently writes for Harlequin's Love Inspired and Heartwarming lines. You can find her at patriciajohnsromance.com.

A Precious Christmas Gift

Patricia Johns

LOVE INSPIRED
INSPIRATIONAL ROMANCE

LOVE INSPIRED®
INSPIRATIONAL ROMANCE

Recycling programs for this product may not exist in your area.

ISBN-13: 978-1-335-48854-1

A Precious Christmas Gift

This edition published by arrangement with Harlequin Books S.A.

For questions and comments about the quality of this book, please contact us at CustomerService@Harlequin.com.

Love Inspired
22 Adelaide St. West, 40th Floor
Toronto, Ontario M5H 4E3, Canada
www.Harlequin.com

Printed in U.S.A.

For I know the thoughts that I think toward you,
saith the Lord, thoughts of peace,
and not of evil, to give you an expected end.
—*Jeremiah* 29:11

To my husband, the best choice I ever made!
And to our son, who makes our family complete.
I love you both.

Chapter One

The wind was bitingly cold this December morning, and Noah Wiebe hunched his shoulders against the probing chill as the Englisher snowplow ground on past Redemption Carpentry. The driver—a man in a baseball cap with cold-reddened ears—nodded at Noah in a silent mutual acknowledgment as the giant blade scraped across the asphalt, snow accumulating in a tumbling avalanche in front of the vehicle. Noah nodded back and headed across the street toward the town center roundabout where Redemption Carpentry had built a nativity stable to collect donations for a local family in need.

Wollie Zook's family, more precisely. Noah had known Wollie since they were both boys, and they'd been good friends. Wollie left the community when he fell in love with an Englisher girl, and when their house went up in flames a week ago, he'd asked for help. He and his wife had four *kinner*, the youngest of which was still a toddler. He was doing his best to provide, and he had a decent job and some insurance, but he needed help to get through the Christmas season. Wollie had been talking to his parents about returning to the Amish life, but whether or not he could make that happen with an Englisher wife and children was anyone's guess. This one had hit Noah hard—but no matter how much Noah liked to get things organized and into line, he wasn't going to be able to help Wollie without the town's cooperation. And Noah had a personal investment in bringing ex-Amish home again.

Noah carried a clapboard sign under one arm, and he stepped aside and politely nodded as an Amish woman with three little girls in tow passed him on the sidewalk. The clapboard had the times that the nativity would be open written in black paint so that passersby would know when to bring the donations that might be in danger of being stolen so that they could be brought back to a safe location. If the Zooks were going to get settled again, they needed everything from forks and spoons up to beds and furniture.

Noah stopped at the top of the street, and then jogged across, ahead of an Amish buggy, heading to the nativity stable in the center. This was his handiwork, and he was proud of it—a traditional looking stable with a locking door and animal silhouette cutouts that decorated the snowy ground in front of it. There was a firepit, too, usually used during street festivals as a source of heat where people could warm up. But today there was no fire in it—just some blackened logs.

Noah paused at the door—it wasn't locked—and when he opened it, he looked into the simple interior and found a woman standing with her back to him, sorting through a box. She looked up as the door thunked open, and when she partially turned, he saw that she was heavily pregnant. She wore a thick, dark gray shawl that seemed to make her creamy skin glow in comparison, and her *kapp* was gleaming white against her dark hair. Her eyes were bright, but she didn't smile. Instead, she turned her attention back to the box.

"Good morning," Noah said.

"Good morning." She pulled out a broken dish and tossed it into another cardboard box, presumably the garbage.

"I'm just here to drop off the sign," he said.

"Oh… Okay. I'm just going through some donations. It's not all good enough to give away." Who was she? She had an interesting face—dark, expressive eyes and a strong jaw. Her lips were pink and they looked perpetually ready to smile, even though she looked at him with a completely solemn expression.

"You're new around here," he said. "Aren't you?"

He was only being polite. Obviously, she was. He knew everyone in their Amish community, and he'd remember meeting a woman like her.

"*Yah*, just visiting," she said.

He nodded. "I'm Noah Wiebe. I work at Redemption Carpentry. I know Wollie Zook, the man we're helping with this charity drive, from our growing up years."

"He's a cousin…on my *mamm*'s side," she said. "A distant one, but still family."

"Oh." Noah nodded. "Well, we'll do our best to get them back on their feet. And you are…"

She blushed slightly. "Sorry. I'm Eve. I'm Lovina Glick's niece."

Noah started. Lovina Glick's niece… His heart sped up as the details clicked into place. Lovina owned Quilts and Such, the shop next door to the carpentry shop, but that wasn't what made his heart skip a beat. This hit his family more personally than even Wollie.

"Wait—" He cleared his throat. "Are you the niece who is…uh…who is…"

Eve turned toward him, her expression wary. Noah now knew exactly who she was. His brother Thomas and his wife Patience were hoping to adopt a baby…

"I'm Thomas Wiebe's brother," he added. "Thomas and Patience Wiebe are… Well, they know your aunt quite well, and…"

How was he supposed to say this? Or had he already said too much? The color drained from Eve's face, and she ran her fingers over her stomach protectively. She suddenly looked different—sadder, even a little smaller.

"*Yah*, that would be me," she said. "I'm the one they're probably hoping to meet."

Noah dropped his gaze. He'd heard a little bit about the mother—a girl who got pregnant outside of wedlock and who had come to give birth to her baby and give it to a good Amish home. There wasn't much more information than that, but Lovina Glick had told Thomas about her niece's baby, and that she hadn't decided on which family she would give her child to. Patience couldn't have any children of her own, and this was a chance to grow their family. It felt like a Christmas answer to prayer…if Eve would choose them, that was.

"Are there any other families you're considering?" Noah asked.

"There is one. They're willing to take the baby, but—" She shrugged. "I don't know. I haven't made up my mind yet."

"Being willing to take a child and longing to take one are two different things," he said.

"Yah." She nodded.

"My brother and his wife—they're longing for another child," he said. "My brother had a child before he met his wife, but they aren't able to have any *kinner* together. They desperately want another baby to grow their family."

She nodded. "It is different, I agree."

Noah smiled at that. Maybe he could put his brother in a good light—help the cause a little bit. Because he knew how deeply Thomas and Patience desired to grow their family.

"I wasn't even going to come here," Eve went on. "Aunt Lovina heard that I was staying with strangers the last few months, and she insisted I come be with family. And when I got here and Wollie's house burned down, I wanted to help him somehow. Wollie was older than me, but he visited us once to help my *daet* with the corn shocks, and he was a good man. I don't know if it's too much to hope he might come back."

"We prayed for him last Service Sunday," he said. "His parents told us that the last time they visited with him, he said he wished he could find a way to come back."

"Really?" Eve's eyebrows went up. "I don't know his *mamm* and *daet* personally. Wollie only visited the once, and he came alone. But that's something to fuel some hope, isn't it?"

"Seems like," he agreed.

Their gazes met and Noah smiled. "Now, I don't like

to blame house fires on *Gott*, but I do believe that *Gott* can use this calamity for good."

"Maybe He will," she agreed.

Noah glanced around. There didn't seem to be anyone else out here. And this was a particularly cold day. Eve rubbed her hands together and blew on her fingers.

"It's cold," he said.

"Yah." She turned back to sorting through the box.

"Are you sure you should be out in this cold—I mean, this close to…" How could he put this delicately?

"Noah…" She paused and turned back. "I could try to be coy about this, but we both know the biggest reason why I'm here in Redemption. I came out here to have my baby and to leave it in the arms of another woman." Her voice shook, and she sucked in a breath. "I've tried not to love this baby—I really have. But I couldn't help it. I love this child, even though I know I have to give it up. So while I wait for that miserable day, I'm trying to make this time count for something— maybe make a difference for Wollie's family in their time of need. This is very likely the hardest thing I will ever do in my lifetime, and the day is coming very quickly. So while I wait, and I dread, are you wanting to take away the one thing that might make this time in your town be about more than my own heartbreak?"

Noah blinked at her. She wasn't like other Amish women—there was no quiet deference to him as a man. But she had a point. He shook his head. "No. I wouldn't do that."

Eve turned back to the box. "Good."

She obviously wasn't looking for permission, nor did she seem overly concerned over his opinion. And yet, looking at her standing there with a donated pot in one hand, she looked very much alone. This was Christmas, and the women would be gathering in warm kitchens to cook together and laugh and talk—

Noah eyed her for a moment. Maybe she didn't have anything more to lose here in Redemption, because she wasn't going out of her way to be friendly, either.

"I know that Thomas and Patience are looking forward to meeting you," he said.

"I'm not ready for that," she replied with a quick shake of her head. She put the pot aside on a folding table and pulled out a teapot next, turning it over as she inspected it.

"Oh…" He wasn't sure what to make of that. Was she perhaps changing her mind about giving up her baby?

"I just need some time," she said, glancing up. "I don't want to meet them until I'm ready."

"No, that's understandable," he said quickly. "And there is no pressure. I promise. In fact, if you need anything at all, you can ask me. I'm Thomas's brother, *yah*, but I'm not quite so directly involved." He cast her a smile, hoping to charm her into relaxing a little bit.

"You're only offering because you want me to choose your brother," she said bluntly.

Noah paused. "Maybe. But I'm going to be around—either at the carpentry shop, or here. And we both want to help Wollie out the best we can, so while we're doing that, if you need anything, tell me."

She licked her lips, then sighed. "Thank you. It's a kind offer. In the meantime, let's do what we can for Wollie."

If she wasn't ready to meet Thomas and Patience

yet, he could understand that. Noah opened the door again to go arrange the sign. He'd start up a little fire in the brick-lined firepit while he was at it, too. But he couldn't help but glance in the direction of the woman with those dark, expressive eyes. There was something about her that tugged at him—and he pushed it aside. This wasn't about him.

Maybe, if *Gott* was willing, this woman could be the answer to Thomas and Patience's most earnest and heartfelt prayers.

Eve sorted through the last of the box—some ladles, three tea towels, a box of matches and a pair of gloves. The rest would be useful, and she pulled out a list her aunt had given her and wrote the items down. They had to keep track of the donations so they would know what else was needed.

But Wollie needed more than household items— he needed to come home to his Amish roots. Just before Wollie jumped the fence, he'd come to help her *daet* with the corn, and she'd been too talkative as a teenager when she'd been doing all the regular adolescent questioning of the Amish ways. When she learned that he'd left the Amish life, she'd been stunned. He seemed so…normal. She'd determined then that she'd never flirt with that line—she'd be good. She'd stay Amish, and have the Amish family she'd always dreamed of.

Her baby shifted and stretched inside her. This far along, there wasn't any room for proper kicks anymore, and she paused her work and put a hand over the spot where the baby was pushing. She could feel something pointy—an elbow?

A wagon came clattering along the road, and she heard the driver's jovial voice as he reined in the horses. Eve looked out the window as Noah headed over to the wagon that was piled high with firewood.

"Hello, Elmer!" Noah called. "Cold enough for you?"

"*Yah*—it's plenty cold," the other voice replied, and when they were close enough, their voices lowered and she could no longer make out what they were saying.

Eve hadn't decided on a family for the baby yet. There were families that would accept another child, but simply being willing to feed and shelter an unwanted baby wasn't what she was hoping for. This baby should be wanted—by someone.

Thomas and Patience seemed like an ideal choice, even though she wasn't ready to admit that to Noah. They wanted this child desperately. And that had made her feel almost competitive with the woman who longed for her baby. It stoked an instinct inside her to fight the woman back. And she knew it wasn't rational. It was maternal instinct—an instinct that she'd have to tamp down. She'd meet this couple eventually, she knew, but she'd been putting it off because she didn't know how she'd feel to look at the woman who might be *mamm* to this baby. She'd rather imagine the baby's adoptive *mamm* like a faceless doll—an idea rather than a real woman who would be everything that Eve could not.

She looked out the window again, watching as the men unloaded wood from the back of that wagon, carrying it over to the firepit and stacking the wood neatly beside it. Noah was taller, broader, and he carried himself with the latent strength of a man accustomed to physical labor. He was distractingly handsome—something that seemed almost silly to be noticing in her present condition—and he might be uncle to this baby.

Adoption was no longer just an idea…she'd be handing her child over to very real people. There would be family, extended family, a whole community—and none of it would include her. So strange to even think that! She'd spent the last eight and a half months being the physical protection for this little one, and when she gave birth, other people would take over. The thought brought a lump of anxiety to her throat.

Noah and Elmer came back to the stable, and when they came in, the older, lanky man looked at her in mild surprise as he saw her figure for the first time. She dropped her gaze and turned away.

"Your husband isn't going to like you being out here in the cold in your state," Elmer said glibly, bending down to pick up a package of matches and kindling that had been stored in a wooden crate in one corner of the small room.

"Let her be," Noah said gruffly. He didn't look up, or explain, but Elmer closed his mouth into a firm line and didn't say anything else.

The men went back out to start a new fire, and the door clattered shut behind them again, leaving her in silence.

She heaved a shaky sigh.

Yes, most Amish assumed she had a husband, because that was how a proper Amish family began— marriage and then babies. She hoped to have that very thing in the next couple of years. She hoped to meet a nice man, marry him, and start a family the respectable way. This child inside her that she was trying so very hard not to get too attached to wasn't even fully Amish. This baby was half-Amish, half-English, and the best way for this baby to grow up would be in a proper Amish home, without the blight of her reputation. To be adopted was in no way shameful. It was a blessing. But to be raised fatherless with an unmarried mother? That was different—that kind of stigma clung.

Outside, she could see that the fire was now started, and Noah hunkered down and poked some wood into the new, crackling flames. She heard the muffled farewell and the clop of horses' hooves as the wagon pulled away.

Eve was done sorting through the latest donations that had been left overnight, and she came back outside toward the fire, leaving the boxed items in the stable for now. She didn't mind admitting that she was cold.

"What did you tell him?" Eve asked, coming up to the flickering warmth.

"That you were visiting your aunt and it was a complicated situation," Noah replied, standing up.

Complicated—that could cover a lot of ground. Was it wrong of her to want people to believe a lie? Because she did! She wanted them to see her as a respectable woman instead of as a warning to the younger girls.

Eve licked her lips. "What are they like?"

"Uh—" Noah looked over at her. "My brother and his wife, you mean?"

"Yah."

"They're very nice. They're newly married—and very much in love. My brother works with me in the carpentry shop. He's very skilled, and his work is in demand with Amish and English alike." Noah crossed his arms over his chest. "My brother had no idea how to be a *daet* when his daughter ended up on his doorstep, but he threw himself into it. I was impressed, really." He glanced toward her. "And it wasn't his fault that he didn't know Rue—that's his little girl. The Englisher *mamm* didn't want him in her life, and what was he supposed to do?"

Eve held her hands out toward the crackling fire. She understood that dilemma well enough, and her aunt had explained Thomas's situation. He'd fathered a child during his *Rumspringa*, and then he and the Englisher mother broke up. The Amish life was separate from the English life—and Amish didn't go about suing others in courts. Thomas would have made his mistake that resulted in a child, and he'd have to live with the painful consequences—much like she would.

"Anyway," Noah went on, "Patience is teaching school until Christmas break, and then her replacement will come and take over. She takes Rue with her some days—so Rue is getting an early start with her reading and writing. She's smart, that little girl. The other days Rue is with her *mammi*, but Patience wants to raise Rue herself, and she wants the girl with her, so…"

"She sounds like she's accepted Rue, then," Eve said. This was a detail that mattered to her.

"Completely."

"Are they strict?" she asked.

Noah paused, then shrugged. "Not overly. Rue managed to keep them from eating a crotchety rooster, just because she loved it."

Eve smiled at that. "That's rather sweet."

"They're good people," Noah said, straightening

to look at her. "And you could be an answer to their prayers—I promise you that. They love *kinner*, and they want nothing more than another baby to raise with Rue."

Eve glanced up as a car sped past. "Lovina said the same."

"Are you… Are you sure that you're willing to give your baby up?" Noah asked.

Was she sure? Not on an emotional level, but she'd thought this through over and over again, and she always landed on the same conclusion.

"I need to find a family for this baby," she said, her throat feeling tight. "That's already decided."

Noah gave a nod, then smiled with a look of relief. "They're good people," he repeated.

And from what she'd heard of them, they were. They'd be loving and stable and faithful. What more could she ask for?

"I will meet your brother and his wife, of course," she added. "Eventually. But right now, I want to find a way to help my cousin."

"Of course." He met her gaze, and her stomach fluttered in response. She looked down.

"I should get back to my aunt's store," she said. "I'm sure she needs some extra help."

Eve just wanted out—away from here. Whatever it was about this man, she was talking too much. She needed to just survive these next couple of weeks—that was all. She could sort out her emotions later, when her future was secured once more. She wrapped her shawl a little more snugly around herself.

"I'd better go," she repeated.

"I'm glad you're here—" he said, then cleared his

throat. "With the charity drive, I mean. I'm glad for another person who sincerely wants to bring Wollie home."

"Yah," she said with a weak smile. "We'll do our best."

Eve met his gaze, and then turned away without any further goodbye. She picked up her pace as she headed across the street and stepped up on the opposite sidewalk, the tiny, icy snowflakes whipping through the air around her.

Noah seemed nice, and he was oddly comforting, but she knew better than to get herself entangled with new friendships while she was here. Eve was in the town of Redemption for one reason, and the Amish community here wasn't going to be any part of her long-term solutions. She was very much in *Gott*'s hands.

Chapter Two

Noah gathered up the box of garbage from the nativity stable and then headed in the same direction Eve had gone, toward Redemption Carpentry. His mind was still on the young woman he'd just met. She wasn't what he'd expected.

In fact, he wasn't sure what he'd expected... Maybe someone who looked more rebellious, but Eve had looked every inch a proper Amish woman. He'd never known anyone in her situation before, and he was personally rather cautious by nature. His brother had had a fairly wild *Rumspringa*, but Noah had all but skipped his own.

He wondered how difficult it must be for Eve being pregnant and single. She seemed like a strong young woman, her personality one that tugged at him in spite of himself. She reminded him a little bit of his own *mamm*, Rachel Wiebe, ironically enough. Not that his *mamm* had ever been in that predicament, but in personality. She hadn't been a typical Amish woman. She used to tell them jokes while she was cooking in the kitchen, and her laughter used to ring through the entire house. Amish women were quiet, and *Mamm* hadn't been quiet at all. But it had been wonderful, and he remembered how happy he used to feel listening to her laughing at her own jokes, completely oblivious to the fact that his own *mamm* was an example of the kind of woman not to marry because she wasn't going to stay.

Rachel Wiebe left the community when he was just a teen, coming back to visit only once a month, and *yah*, he was angry about that. Her weekly letters didn't take the place of her presence, and he hadn't been willing to go join her with his aunt and English cousins, no matter how many times she begged him to. But it wasn't just his *mamm* going English that was so upsetting. He was angrier still that the way she'd raised them had stuck— both the Amish teaching and the laughing and joking, and he found himself drawn to Amish women with a similar personality. That was problematic, because while he'd learned later just how un-Amish his *mamm* had been, he couldn't help the type of woman who drew him in. Like the pregnant woman in the stable— outspoken, direct. And that wasn't helpful to him at all.

Noah let himself into the carpentry shop showroom and took off his hat, slapping it against his thigh to shake off the snow. The customer side of the shop was empty, and his brother was leaning over some paperwork at the counter.

"You'll never believe who I saw in the charity stable," Noah said.

Thomas raised his eyebrows questioningly.

"Eve," Noah said. "Lovina's niece. She's arrived."

"Eve… The mother?" Thomas asked, straightening. "She's in the stable?"

"She was. She's in Quilts and Such with Lovina at the moment," Noah said.

"Did you talk to her?" Thomas asked.

"*Yah*, we chatted a bit," Noah confirmed. "I made sure to talk you up a bit, tell her what a great *daet* you are."

"I should go say hello," Thomas said, wiping his hands down the sides of his pants. "Patience should be with me for this, but—"

"Look," Noah said. "She said she isn't ready to meet you yet."

"Why?" Thomas asked. "Lovina says she's due by Christmas."

"I don't know," Noah replied. "And she said it's hard to think about giving up her baby, and she needs some time before she meets you."

"Is there another family she's considering, or something?"

"There is one other that she mentioned," he replied.

"I didn't know there was another one." Thomas rubbed a hand over his short, reddish beard, then looked up at Noah. "I thought we were it."

"*Yah*, that's the impression I got from Lovina, too," Noah agreed. "But I guess there is one more."

Thomas sighed. "When Lovina said she'd told her niece about us, you should have seen Patience's face. She just…glowed. I don't know… I just know that Patience and I are going to have more *kinner* in our home, and Patience deserves a baby in her arms. She does. She's a wonderful *mamm*, and…maybe I shouldn't have gotten her hopes up. I really thought this was more certain than it seems to be."

"Yah..." Noah didn't know how to answer that.

"I don't want to overstep with Eve," Thomas said. "And I can appreciate how difficult this would be for her, but maybe she'll need something that we can provide. I don't mean it as pressure, but as Christian charity."

"I offered, actually," Noah said. "I hope I wasn't going too far on your behalf, but when she said she wasn't ready to meet you, I thought maybe she'd accept it from me. I'm not quite so personally involved."

Thomas hooked his thumb into the front of his pants and sighed. He looked worried.

"Sometimes the *mamm* changes her mind," Thomas said after a pause. "It happens, you know. The *mamm* decides to keep the baby, or she chooses a different family."

That was the fear—Noah knew it. Thomas and Patience had already gotten their hopes up, and it had all felt a little too perfect. It had felt like *Gott* was moving... A half-Englisher baby in need of an Amish home.

"Thomas, she said she's looking for a family for the baby, so..." Noah shrugged helplessly. "Besides, I'll be seeing more of her. She's one of Wollie's distant cousins. So she's invested in helping his family right now."

The door to the shop opened again, and Amos Lapp, the owner of Redemption Carpentry, came into the showroom. He wiped some wood dust from the hair on his arms and looked between them curiously. Amos was nearing forty, and there was some gray at his temples and just a few strands in his beard, but he was tall and strong.

"What?" Amos asked. "You both look like something's happened."

Noah retold the story of his brief encounter with Eve in the charity stable, and Amos blew out a slow breath. Amos had taken Noah and Thomas into his home when they were teens, and of anyone in Redemption, Amos understood them best.

"Should I just go introduce myself?" Thomas asked. "I mean...if she sees me and meets Patience, maybe it will take away her anxiety. We'll love her baby. We've already gotten attached, I think. If she could see—"

"Don't push her," Amos interrupted.

"I'm not suggesting I overstep, exactly—" Thomas began.

"I didn't think I was overstepping with Miriam, either," Amos replied.

Noah froze and exchanged a glance with his brother. Amos didn't talk about his wife often. All they knew was that they had broken up after less than a year of marriage. She'd gone back to her hometown, and they'd both continued with their lives alone. It took a lot to break up an Amish couple, because there was no remarriage for them unless their spouse died. But Miriam Lapp had gone home, and she'd never returned to her husband.

"What happened between you and Miriam, exactly?" Noah asked.

"You could say she was stubborn and unyielding. You could say I was just the same. But one of the mistakes I made, looking back on it, was that I didn't take her seriously enough. When a woman looks you in the eye and says something, she means it." Amos shuffled his feet uncomfortably. "Women are…different. They're both stronger than us and more fragile. So if she's said that she isn't ready to meet Thomas and Patience yet, my humble advice is that you take that woman at her word. Give it a few days."

"Yah…" Thomas licked his lips. "That makes sense. I should ask Patience what she thinks, all the same, but you're probably right."

It wasn't like any of them had a wealth of experience when it came to women. Amos had been estranged from his wife for nearly ten years. Noah was single, and Thomas had been married for all of three months. All combined, they weren't exactly experts in the female mind. Waiting for Patience to give an opinion was probably the smartest thing to be done. She had just as much at stake as her husband, after all.

Thomas went back into the workshop, and Noah exchanged a look with Amos.

"You never told us much about Miriam," Noah said.

"I don't want to scare you off of marriage," Amos said. "Choose a quiet, hardworking woman, and you'll be fine. Don't overreach. That's all. It's simple enough."

Noah smiled ruefully. "Have you ever thought of going to get her? Bringing her home once and for all?"

"I tried," Amos replied. "It didn't go well."

Amos didn't look amused, and Noah let his smile fall.

"We should get back to work," Noah said.

"Yah. There are orders to complete," Amos agreed.

There was one complete bedroom set that needed sanding still, and three different hutches that had been

ordered in the last few weeks that were still in the beginning stages of the work. Redemption Carpentry was
known for its quality work, but also for keeping to its
promised delivery dates.

When the bell dinged from the customer showroom,
Noah had just finished rubbing oil into the side of a
newly finished bedside table, and he dropped the rag
on his workbench and headed toward the door, letting
Amos and Thomas continue undisturbed.

When Noah stepped into the showroom, it wasn't an
Englisher client as expected, but Lovina Glick. Noah
looked at her in surprise.

"Hi, Lovina," he said.

"Hello." Lovina smiled. "Is it a busy day today?"

"Well, we keep pretty steady," Noah replied. "It is
Christmas."

Lovina nodded knowingly. "It's the same with my
shop, and add in trying to organize the charity drive
for Wollie's family..."

"*Yah*, I saw your niece there today."

"I'm glad it's you who came out." Lovina lowered
her voice. "You see, I need to go check on my mother.
She and my aunt have been working on more quilts
for me to sell, and we need to pick them up. I'm a little
worried—my aunt was supposed to bring them to the
shop first thing in the morning."

"Do you think they're sick, or—"

"I'm sure they're fine, but I won't feel better until
I check."

"That's understandable," Noah agreed.

"Eve is minding the shop for me while I'm gone, but
if I don't come back in time, I was wondering if you

might be able to drop her off at our house when you leave for the day. I don't want her to be too tired out in her condition."

"*Yah*, that wouldn't be a problem. It's on the way," Noah replied.

"I…" Lovina smiled apologetically. "She isn't ready for a proper meeting with Thomas yet."

"She mentioned that, and Thomas understands."

"Good." Lovina smiled again. "Thank you. I do appreciate it, especially at this busy time. And don't worry about Eve not wanting to meet your brother just yet. She just needs some time to adjust."

"What are neighbors for?" Noah asked.

"Thank you," Lovina said again. "I'd better go, then."

"*Yah*—say hello to your *mamm* for me."

"I will. She'll be tickled you thought of her." Lovina smiled, her eyes crinkling at the corners and her entire face softening.

With a wave, she swept back out the front door, the bell dinging over her head. As Lovina headed out, an Englisher woman came inside, pulling her gloves off. She was dressed in blue jeans and a bright red coat that matched her lipstick.

"Hello!" she said. "I'm looking for something for a Christmas gift for my mother—"

Yes, Christmas brought out the urgent requests for everything from quilt racks to full shelving units. And staying busy was a blessing to any business.

Noah glanced toward the door once more, his mind moving to the young woman in the shop next door. Eve was vulnerable, but she seemed so determined to take care of herself. At a time like this, a woman needed a husband to be caring for her...

"...I was hoping for a medium-size one," the woman was saying, and Noah realized he'd tuned out.

"Sorry," he said. "Could you repeat that?"

"A spice rack, but I wanted something with an Amish flair to it, you know?"

Noah blinked at her. "Maybe some Pennsylvania Dutch on it?"

"Yes, that would be perfect! How do you say 'kiss the cook' in Pennsylvania Dutch?"

Not exactly an Amish flair. Noah swallowed. "How about something like '*Gott* bless this home'?" he asked.

"Oh...yes, that might do," she replied. "How long will that take to make? I need it in time for Christmas. Did I say that already?"

Christmas. It brought out the Englishers, but it also brought out thoughts of friends, family and goodwill. There was his brother, Thomas, and his hopes for another child. There was Wollie, who had lost everything in that fire, but who was still in *Gott*'s hands. And there was Noah's *mamm*, who had returned to Redemption as an answer to his own prayer...but in spite of all of *Gott*'s goodness, Noah was missing some necessary element in his life to make him feel rooted and satisfied, and he knew what he needed. A wife. He needed a family of his own, like his brother now had. But he wasn't sure he trusted himself to find a woman who wouldn't break his heart.

Marriage was for life, and if a man married the wrong woman, heartbreak was for life, too. Just ask Amos.

Gott, *help me stay on the narrow path.*

* * *

Eve looked at her watch. It was time to close up Quilts and Such, and Aunt Lovina still hadn't returned. The last few customers had been Amish, and they'd asked a few questions about where she was from. This visit would be simpler if Eve could just keep to herself, spend time with the Glick family and not see another person, but *Gott* wasn't leaving her with that option. She had to admit that sitting by herself, feeling the nudges and movements of her baby inside her, wouldn't make these last few weeks any easier. Part of her wanted to get this over with—have her baby, and just face the pain of giving the child up. And another part of her wished she'd never have to face it—that she could go on forever with this little one inside her, feeling those jabs and movements with no one to separate them.

But nothing lasted forever, especially not a pregnancy.

The shop had been picked over today—a few rolls of fabric had gone from fat and full to nearly empty, and almost all of the Christmas crafts that women from the community made and brought to the quilt shop to sell had been purchased by one of the many Englisher shoppers. There had been little log cabin tree ornaments, snowflake-decorated aprons, embroidered oven mitts, and one enterprising Amish family had been making little Amish Christmas villages that sold for a very good price. There had only been four of them, and more than one customer had asked after them once they were sold.

The most difficult part of the evening was the questions—not from the Amish customers, but from the English. *Oh, when are you due? Boy or girl?* And then added with a lowered voice, *Do you people find out the gender, or is that considered Fancy?*

Eve flicked the sign in the frost-laced front window from Open to Closed. It was a painted sign that was made to look like the words had been cross-stitched. She turned to the front door and was about to flick the lock, too, when Noah appeared on the other side of the glass. She startled—she hadn't seen him come up in the winter evening darkness and he materialized all at once, his thick woolen black coat and rimmed hat blending into the darkness behind him. He held a pair of gloves in one hand, and he smiled hesitantly. Eve pulled the door open and let him inside. He eased past her, and she noticed how tall he was next to her, and broad. She turned the lock behind him.

"I was just closing up," Eve said. "Thank you for the ride home. I really appreciate it."

"So Lovina didn't make it back?" he asked.

"Lovina said that her *mamm* might need help with a few things," Eve replied. "She thought it might take some time."

"Right." He nodded, glanced around. "Are you ready to leave?"

"Almost." Eve didn't know how to deal with the cash or do the paperwork for end of day, and Lovina had told her not to worry about that since they could take care of it in the morning. She straightened a bin of thread spools and ran a duster over the counter. Noah stood to one side, fiddling with his gloves, and she noticed as she glanced around the store one last time that his dark eyes were locked on her. When she met his gaze, he dropped his immediately.

Eve had a coat—one she was borrowing from Lovina's husband—that was big enough to cover her belly. She reached for it, and when she fumbled with the heavy woolen garment, Noah stepped forward and caught it, holding it open for her to slide her arms into.

"Thank you." She felt her cheeks warm. "It's heavy."

"Yah." He caught her eye, and she saw warmth in that smile—something she wasn't used to lately. In the last community where she'd been staying, the Amish there all knew she was "one of those girls," and there wasn't much friendliness. Kindness, yes, but friendliness was a different sort of thing. Even the older woman she'd stayed with had been emotionally removed—offering food, clothing, shelter and spiritual guidance, but not friendliness.

Eve's feet were sore. Lovina had provided a chair for her to sit in, but it didn't seem to take much to make her feet ache in these last few weeks. She took off her indoor shoes and slipped her feet into her winter boots, then she picked up a bag of scraps her aunt had said she could have. They headed for the back door that lead through the storage room and then out into the brisk cold air. Eve paused to lock the door with the key Lovina had entrusted to her, and then they headed to the waiting buggy. Noah had already hitched up the horses, and she accepted his work-roughened hand as he helped her up into the buggy. He didn't let go of her hand in his tight grip until she was seated, and then he released her and headed around the horses to the other side.

Eve picked up a lap blanket and tucked it around her knees. Dresses, even with lots of layers underneath them, were cold this time of year. She let out a slow breath that hung in the air in front of her. The stars shone bright, and a full moon illuminated the sky. Streetlights lit up the parking lot, and the horses shifted their hooves on the snowy asphalt. As Noah hoisted himself up into the seat beside her, he gave her a reassuring smile.

"Was it busy today?" he asked as he flicked the reins, the horses starting forward and heading toward the road without any further encouragement from Noah.

"*Yah*—lots of shoppers," she said. "Lots of questions from them, too."

"You mentioned keeping the adoption discreet," he said. "Have people pieced it together?"

"I'm not sure. Maybe a few. I'm only saying that I'm here to see my aunt, and most have been too polite to pry much further. The thing is, I'd like a life still when I go home. I'd like a chance at marriage and being a proper part of the community."

He didn't answer, and she thought she knew what he was thinking—it was the very thing she'd be thinking, too, in his shoes. Did she even deserve that second chance? They rolled out onto the street and through the downtown, the horses plodding along through the sound-dampening snow on the roads. Eve pulled the blanket up a little higher and put her hands under the woolen folds.

"This wasn't my fault," she added. "This…pregnancy. I didn't do wrong, you know."

Noah looked over at her, perplexed.

"It was a party," she said, saving him the discomfort. "I took my *Rumspringa* late. When I was seventeen, I was taking care of my *mamm* while she battled cancer.

When she died, I took my *Rumspringa*, and it wasn't a rebellious one, either. But I went to an Englisher party with some other Amish girls, and someone must have put something in my drink, because I woke up the next morning on a couch and I couldn't remember what happened."

"Your friends left you there?" he asked.

"They thought I'd left early. I said I was going to. It was too wild. It scared me. But then I accepted a drink, and... I don't know. I must have passed out."

"I've heard some boys can do that," he said gruffly.

"An Englisher taxi brought me home for free—the driver was a woman and she felt sorry for me, I guess. When I found out I was pregnant, I knew where it had happened, but I couldn't even remember what those Englisher boys looked like. It was all so fuzzy."

"That's horrible!" Noah's tone hardened. "No one went to try to figure it out?"

"My *daet* and I had a long talk, and we decided that we'd deal with things as they were rather than try to get some justice."

"Your community would understand, though," he said.

"As much as they could." Because while they might not blame her, she would certainly be in an outside circle. She'd gone to the party, after all, and she hadn't done the right thing and left immediately for home. She'd lingered, wondering if she was overreacting. She'd talked to the Englisher boys, and she'd enjoyed that strange feeling of freedom she'd never experienced before.

No, if she'd told her community what had happened,

they wouldn't have blamed her, but they'd never forget, either. She certainly wouldn't have been marriageable when there were so many other girls available without babies already.

"It would be complicated, though," Noah said, and she was glad to have him see that fact instead of having him argue with her about it. It wasn't like she hadn't agonized about this choice for the last several months.

Noah flicked the reins, and the horses picked up their pace, the buggy moving slowly around the roundabout and the little nativity stable that sat in the center. There were some bags placed in front—more donations since they'd last been there, it seemed. With the animal outlines in front, the blanket of fresh snow surrounding it, and the warm bath of a streetlight beaming down, the scene looked so simple and festive that it brought a wave of nostalgia for her own Christmases past. But those happy times when her *mamm* was alive weren't coming back.

"What was your *Rumspringa* like?" she asked.

"Uneventful," he replied. "I was working at the shop, and I was wanting to build my career, not take a break from it."

She nodded. That was the ideal, actually—a *Rumspringa* that allowed an Amish young person to see the English life without too much drama involved. She'd wanted to enjoy herself, though—see what all the fuss was about. She'd never dreamed she'd be in this position.

"You're a hard worker," she said.

"Yah," he agreed. "It seems like a good use of time."

She shot him a rueful look. Yes, she knew his type

well. He was the kind of man who got ahead, and who could be relied upon to stand by his word. But he was also single—she knew it from his shaved face. Maybe there was a girlfriend.

"Are you saving for a wedding?" she asked.

He looked over at her, and color touched his cheeks. "No."

"Okay." She chuckled. "I didn't mean to overstep, it's just—you seem to have your life in order, and most men are moving on to finding a wife."

"A wife isn't so easy to find," he said.

"Around here? I'm sure there are plenty of single girls," she replied. "Even Wollie found one."

But Noah didn't smile.

"He married an Englisher. And it's ruined his life," he replied.

"*Yah*… I was…joking," she said feebly.

"Oh." He shrugged and gave her an apologetic look. "Sorry. I can get too serious sometimes. I guess I'm just being careful. That's a decision you have to get right the first time."

And somehow she didn't doubt him. He would be cautious—and he *could* be. He had a lot to offer a woman in these parts.

"I'm sorry about your *mamm*," Noah added.

Eve looked over at him in mild surprise. She'd told her story in the other community, and Noah was the first one to say that. Everyone else had been too fixated on her pregnancy and what it would mean for her future.

"*Yah*…" she said quietly.

"When did she pass?" Noah asked.

"Just after Christmas last year. She was sick for about three years. She fought hard, but…"

That was another reason she just wanted to get past this Christmas—she'd lost her *mamm*, and in a very real way over the next few months, she'd gone from cherished girl to woman in an awkward, jolting dash. Normally, that milestone happened with marriage for an Amish girl, but enough heartbreak could have the same effect, she realized. She'd grown up, just not in a way her community could acknowledge.

They'd moved outside of the town center, and the streetlights grew farther apart as they headed toward the dark, rural streets. The headlamps illuminated the backs of the horses and the road ahead, the horses' shadows stretching out in front of them. A car slowed and passed them, giving a good distance around the buggy, but it still made Eve's heart jump.

"You had to grow up fast," he said.

"Yah," she agreed. "When *Mamm* got sick, I had to take over most of the housework for months at a time. I was keeping house on my own, helping *Mamm* take her medication and selling extra produce plus anything that wasn't nailed down so we could get extra money for *Mamm*'s treatments."

"That's not easy," he said.

Before she died, her mother had tried to tell her something. Eve could still remember the earnestness in her mother's gaze, the way she'd clutched at Eve's fingers. It was like she wanted something from Eve— a promise? "I did my best, Eve," her mother had whispered. "I did." Did she somehow know what was to come—her daughter's pregnancy out of wedlock?

Those last words now felt like an accusation. This was not the life her mother had wanted for her.

"Did you envy the girls who didn't have to grow up so fast?" Noah asked, and she pushed the memory back.

"Yah." She looked away. "Maybe that was why I went to that party to begin with. I wanted a break from all the pressure. I wanted to just have fun for a change…"

"That's understandable," he said.

"Is it?" she asked softly, and she ran her hand over her belly.

"I understand having to grow up really quickly," he said. "My *daet* died when I was fifteen."

"I'm sorry. That's a tough age to lose your *daet*."

"It was hard," he said. "And I became the man of the house overnight. I had just graduated from the eighth grade, and I had to start giving my *mamm* the money I made at Amos's shop to pay the bills. I was expecting to work full-time, but I didn't realize how fast the money went once you had to pay for everything."

"So you grew up fast, too," she said.

"Yah," he agreed. "But I still think back on what it was like when *Daet* was alive and we had our family. Those were more precious times than I realized back then."

"What were your parents like?" she asked. "Together, I mean… Were they happy?"

"Yah," he said, thinking back. "They laughed a lot when they were together. And when they felt uncomfortable in any way, they leaned toward each other. Like, physically. You could see it. Both of them. When *Daet* died, my mom had no one to lean toward anymore."

Eve smiled sadly. "They sound like they were well matched."

"How about yours?" he asked.

"Not so well matched," she admitted. "There wasn't much laughing. At least not when they were together."

"There's nothing wrong with being more serious," he said.

"Well, *Daet* is serious—very stoic and pious," she said. "He insisted upon family worship at the same time every evening, no matter what was happening. *Mamm* was the fun one. She told jokes and found the light side of life, but that only seemed to irritate *Daet*. He thought she was pulling us *kinner* away from more serious concerns."

"My *mamm* was like that, too," he said.

"But your *daet* liked her humor," she countered.

Noah seemed to consider a moment, then nodded. "*Yah*, he did. But yours—they weren't happy?"

"I think they tried to be," she said. "But they were too different. She drove him up the wall with her jokes and how she could be late sometimes. And he exasperated her with his refusal to budge, even an inch, on something he'd told us *kinner* to do." She let out a slow breath. "They were *so* different."

"That's too bad," he said.

"It got better, though," she said. "I don't mean to make it sound like we weren't a happy family. When *Mamm* got sick, *Daet* softened up a lot. I think he appreciated her more when he knew he was going to lose her."

"Is he softer now?" Noah asked.

"He's…" Eve tried to find the words to describe her father. "Let's just say that he's trying."

It made her guilty to even think it, but they were happier when *Mamm* was sick. Everyone worked harder at being kinder to each other and making sure that *Mamm* was comfortable and didn't need to get upset about anything.

"I think that trying matters," Noah said.

"It does, but it's not always enough," she said quietly.

Noah nodded. *"Yah..."*

"But enough about my family," she said, forcing a smile. "What do you do for fun around here?"

"Me?" Noah smiled faintly. "Like I said before, I work."

"That's it?" she asked.

"Well, I like what I do," he replied. "And there's always more that needs to be done. Since I don't have a family of my own, I have the time."

"You're the stoic, pious one, aren't you?" she asked with a soft laugh.

"I think I am," he said, but a smile tickled his lips. "It's just my personality, I'm afraid."

"That can't be helped," she replied.

Eve turned her attention to the snowy fields—the glitter of moonlight reflecting off the crust of snow. Barbed-wire fences cut through like stitches on a patchwork quilt.

"When Wollie married that Englisher girl, none of us could see why he did it," Noah said quietly. "I still wonder... What was he thinking?"

Everyone at her home had asked the same question—why would he do that? But Eve knew something that most of them didn't...

"He came to help my *daet* with the corn shocks just

before he jumped the fence," Eve said. "And I used to follow him around and talk to him. One of the things he told me a few times—enough times that I remember it today—was that it was important to do the right thing, even when you'd made a mistake. He said that two wrongs didn't make a right. And three wrongs just made it all worse. So I know he was noble, and honest. I've thought about what he said a lot over the last few months."

"Doing the right thing, even after a mistake?" Noah asked quietly.

"*Yah*. I think this is right—giving a family a child to raise. It hurts deeply to do it, but the right thing often does, doesn't it? I made a mistake in not leaving that party right away, but compounding that mistake with my own selfishness will only punish this child. An unwed mother... Can you imagine growing up Amish with that stigma?"

"I can't answer that for you," Noah said.

"My *daet* overpaid Wollie by a few dollars when it was time for him to leave, and Wollie counted it out and handed back the extra. My *daet* was impressed with him. Wollie was...a good man. When he left the Amish life like that, everyone thought he'd just succumbed to temptation, but I don't. Sometimes there's more to the story—I know that better than most."

"He left for an Englisher girl," he said. "That's what we all assumed, at least. He married her shortly after."

"That wouldn't have been noble, though," she said. "Do you think I'm naive for still believing the best in him?"

Noah shrugged. "I think it says more about you than it does about him."

They fell silent, and Eve looked out the side of the buggy, watching the snowy fields glisten in the passing light of their headlamps. What did it say about her—that for all her quick growing up, she was still very much a girl in some ways? She wasn't sure. Maybe she just wanted to believe that people could be good at heart, even after a big mistake. Maybe she wanted to believe in redemption.

"I like you," Noah said after a moment. "You're honest, too."

She smiled at that—his confession had been unexpected. Well, she liked him, too, in spite of all his seriousness, but she wouldn't tell him that.

"This is my last chance to be completely open," she said, attempting a joke. "Maybe I'm relishing it a little. After this I'll have nothing but secrets."

Chapter Three

The Glick house was only a couple of miles away from the house Noah shared with Amos and Amos's elderly grandmother who they fondly referred to as *Mammi*. He guided the horses down the drive, leaving the cold, dark road behind. They pulled up to the warmly lit house, and he could see the white *kapp* of a girl in the window—her back to them. The windows that he could see were all decorated with evergreen sprigs, red ribbons tying them together, and candles that flickered on the windowsills. It was homey, and festive in the Amish way.

"Here we are," Noah said.

"Yah." Eve leaned forward to look at the house. "Thank you for the ride."

Noah brought the horses to a stop and tied off the reins. Eve moved toward the side of the buggy, the plastic bag in one hand, then hesitated.

"I can't see my feet anymore," she said with a low laugh.

"Wait—just wait." Noah hopped down into the

crunchy snow and headed around the horses to her side of the buggy. Eve's face looked so pale, even partially lit by the golden glow of the buggy's headlamp. She must be tired, he realized belatedly. Should he have picked her up sooner to bring her home?

"Here—" He held his hand up and she caught his fingers in hers, then leaned into his shoulder as she maneuvered herself down. There was something about the softness of her in his arms—even though she was all coat, and all he grabbed were her arms, but still… She smelled like the nutmeg and cinnamon scent that filled the fabric store this time of year mingled with the soft scent of her hair. That plastic bag rustled against his coat. He waited until she had her balance on the snowy ground, then let out a breath.

"Sorry," she said, pulling free of his grip. "I feel so ungraceful."

"Don't be sorry." If things had been different for her, this would be a husband's role. She didn't have that, and it wasn't her fault. At least he knew that now. He still felt an angry tangle of emotions knowing what had happened to her. Someone should have paid for that—even if making your enemy pay went against everything he believed in.

"I do appreciate the ride home, and the conversation. But you don't have to do this, you know," Eve said.

"What?" he asked. Helping her down?

"Being friendly, entertaining me," she replied. "I don't need to be someone's Christian duty."

"You're not. You're… Well, you're connected to us, in a way," he said.

"If you're being kind to me because you want me to choose Thomas and Patience—"

"*Yah*, I do hope that you choose them, and I'll probably tell you how great they'd be as parents a few more times yet, but…this isn't about my brother."

"No?"

He'd already opened up more on this ride home than he ever had with a girl before. It had started as wanting her to be comfortable with their family, but…

"Honestly? Christmas isn't an easy time for me," he said. "You aren't the only one trying to get through, although you've got it worse than me, I'll readily admit."

"Are you saying you…need a friend?" she asked uncertainly.

"I wouldn't turn one down," he replied.

A smile came to her lips, and for the first time she seemed to relax, and the smile transformed her face from pretty to downright stunning. He caught his breath.

"I'm going to be dropping off some food at the hotel where Wollie is staying tomorrow," he added. "Do you want to come along?"

"Uh—" She hesitated. "*Yah*. I do. Thank you."

"Great. I'll come by and pick you up, then."

Eve turned toward the side door, and Noah followed her. When she opened it, the sound of laughter and the scent of baking wafted out together to meet him. One of Lovina's daughters waved at him with a smile.

"Hi, Noah! Why don't you come in for some apple crisp? We have it fresh from the oven."

The sweet aroma curled around him where he stood on the step, but he shook his head. Eve wanted to get in and get warm, and he needed to get home. *Mammi* would have a meal waiting.

"Thanks for the offer," Noah said. "But when I get home, *Mammi* is going to be deeply offended if I don't eat dinner. I'd better get going."

He waved at the teenage boys who looked out to see who was there, and then he looked back at Eve and met her gaze.

"Thank you," she said so quietly that he didn't hear it, but he could see the words formed on her lips.

He didn't answer, but gave her another nod. Now that he'd seen that smile, there was no forgetting it, and as he headed back to the buggy, he had to remind himself that this was supposed to be about Thomas and Patience, and their hope for a baby. Because they all did hope that she would choose Thomas and Patience, after all. Dropping her off to her family's home, waving to her cousins and seeing himself off again—*yah*, all of that had felt a little too familiar, and it left him with an unsettled feeling in his stomach.

Noah turned the buggy around and the horses took him back down the drive to the road, and they headed in the direction of home.

Right now, in the midst of the Christmas bustle, Noah was looking for a little bit of peace of his own. He was hoping that Wollie would find a place in their community again, and that Eve would give her baby to Thomas and Patience. And he was hoping that he'd find what he was looking for, too—some peace that seemed so elusive lately.

The winter wind whisked into the open buggy window, nipping at his ears and nose. The Glicks' Englisher neighbors had their Christmas lights up along the eaves of their house, and there were plastic reindeer in the yard, lights coiled around their bodies.

This Christmas his *mamm* was properly back in the Amish life for the first Christmas season in a very long time, and he found himself working his fingers to the bone at the workshop, in the charity drive for Wollie, and even to gain the good opinion of this young mother—anything but face his own feelings surrounding his mother. His prayer of the last ten years had been answered. He was supposed to be happy, but Noah hadn't counted on forgiving his own mother being quite this difficult.

Aunt Lovina came back home in time to eat dinner together as a family, and then the boys went to the sitting room to talk and read *The Budget*. Uncle Hezekiah, who was working a night shift at the canning plant, headed upstairs for an early bedtime since he'd be up in a few hours to get to work.

Eve had been thinking about Noah, and how he was oddly comforting in his own gruff, serious way. It wasn't just his kindness or his good looks, either, she realized. He was more familiar than she'd realized at first—he was a lot like her father. *Daet* was serious and dedicated to doing the right thing, too. He was the kind of man a neighbor could count on—the kind of man who made an Amish community work. But he'd also opened her eyes to what a good man wanted in a wife.

"When I was courting your *mamm*," he'd told her, "I was watching for her character. I knew I wanted to marry her, but I also wanted to make sure she was the woman I thought she was. Before we announced the engagement, a man from another community came to ours to look for a wife, and he set his eyes on your mother. He even told me that he thought she was beautiful, and I didn't tell him she was mine."

"That wasn't fair, *Daet*," Eve used to say with a laugh. "The poor man! Making a fool of himself..."

"I wanted to see what your *mamm* would do." He always told the story in the same way. "And she told him straightaway that she was spoken for, and she wished him well. I knew then that she was a woman I could trust with my heart and my good name."

Good men were looking for good women, and they had a lot to lose if they miscalculated. As did a woman, for that matter! If her mother had entertained that other man's attention, Eve's *daet* would have called the engagement off. That was all it would have taken.

What about a girl with a baby? Who would take a chance on that? Not a good man. The good ones would be careful—much like Noah was doing.

It was times like this that her mother's last words would come back to her... *I did my best, Eve...* And Eve had let her mother down.

Whatever warm feelings he'd brought up for her on that buggy ride back, she'd best quash them now. Her situation was too complicated. When she went back home again, when her secret was safely tucked in another woman's arms in Redemption, then she could allow herself to enjoy a good man's company.

After dinner, Eve had helped her two cousins, Ruby and Rebecca, along with Lovina in cleaning up the kitchen. With four of them working, it went quickly.

The girls were kind enough to Eve, but there was a careful refusal to even mention Eve's condition.

That was the most tiring part of this whole ordeal—the humiliation of her pregnancy. Her cousins chatted with her cordially enough, but they never asked about the baby, or about how she was feeling, or even asked to feel the baby kick. If Eve stopped drying dishes and put her hand over a spot where the baby was kicking, they'd turn away and pretend not to see as if it were shameful, somehow.

But they were young—fifteen and sixteen respectively—so they were doing what they'd been taught to do, namely, keep to the narrow way. If anything, Eve was an example of what to avoid—a cautionary tale for their own upcoming *Rumspringas*, but ironically enough, Eve was not allowed to tell her own story. She could only stand there as a swollen representation of all their fears, and Eve hated it. But what could she do?

When the counters were wiped down and the last dish had been put away, the girls went to join their brothers in the sitting room, leaving Eve alone with her aunt.

"Have you seen Wollie at all?" Eve asked. "I mean, recently."

"Yah," Lovina replied. "Their insurance company is paying for them to stay in a hotel for now. I think there is some tension between Wollie and his parents, so I invited the family to come stay with us for the holidays, but the hotel is…more comfortable for an English woman, I suppose."

Eve could sense her aunt's hurt feelings.

"How is he?" Eve asked. "I mean, besides the fire."

"He's the same old Wollie," Lovina said. "I mean, he looks English now, but he's the same in the ways that matter."

Looking English—even thinking of Wollie dressed like that made her uncomfortable.

"And his wife?" Eve asked.

"His wife is overwrought by everything," Lovina replied. "And she seemed wary of us. I know that Wollie said he was thinking of coming back, but there is no changing one mind in a couple. You have to convince both, or give up."

There was wisdom there, but it made Eve's heart sink. Had things gone too far for Wollie to return?

"Noah offered to bring me along to drop off some food at the hotel tomorrow," Eve said. "Can I trust Wollie to keep my secret?"

Lovina was silent for a moment, considering. "He's English now. He isn't passing gossip around with the community at large."

"I know, but—" This was sensitive—more than that, this secret was about her chance at a future.

"If you can trust me, then I think you can trust Wollie," Lovina said. "Besides, who knows? Maybe you're the one Wollie needs to see."

Eve nodded. Maybe her aunt was right—there might be more divine design in the timing of her visit and his time of need.

"I thought you'd be tired," Lovina said, hanging up a tea towel. "When I was as pregnant as you are, I'd crawl into bed just as soon as I could."

"I am tired," Eve admitted. "But I wanted to do a little bit of quilting tonight."

"For Wollie's family?" Lovina asked. "I think I have enough quilts set aside for them, but you know it is winter—an extra blanket is always useful. Don't worry about making it too intricate—"

No, this one would be more personal. Eve licked her lips.

"I wanted to make something for the baby," Eve said.

Lovina froze, then slowly pursed her lips. "You've changed your mind, then?"

Eve blinked, then shook her head. "No…"

"Then why are you making something for the baby?" Lovina asked.

"Because I wanted to make something to go along with him or her—something from me. Maybe this little quilt would end up being my child's favorite blanket, and it would get dragged all over the house and outside, and—" Her voice cracked as tears rose in her eyes. Maybe there could be some tangible way that her love could go along with this baby to a new home. Maybe this welling of love she felt for the squirming baby inside her needn't be wasted.

"Sit." Lovina gestured to a kitchen chair.

"Lovina, I'm not in the mood to be lectured," Eve replied with a shake of her head. Yes, she was unmarried and pregnant, and yes, she was in the very situation that Ruby and Rebecca were being warned about constantly, but Eve was the one who would have to bear the heartrending consequences of her assaulter's actions, and that was punishment enough.

"I said, sit." Lovina raised her eyebrows, and Eve couldn't resist the command in the older woman's voice. She pulled out a chair and sat down. Lovina sighed, then pulled out the chair next to her and sank into it. "I know it's hard."

Eve looked over at her aunt uncertainly. "And this is where you tell me that I'm doing the right thing and I need to just toughen up and do it, right?"

Lovina shook her head slowly. "Not at all. I just know that this is hard. And maybe I haven't had the chance to tell you that yet."

Eve hadn't wanted a lecture, but sympathy might be worse. She wiped at a tear that escaped her lashes. "Have you ever given up a child?"

"No," Lovina said quietly.

"It's harder than you'd even imagine it to be," Eve said, her voice thick. The baby squirmed, and she ran a hand over her belly tenderly.

"If you want my humble opinion, sending a gift along with the baby is a kind gesture, but it won't make it easier for the child. Let the baby go to that family fully and completely. Let the *mamm* raise this baby as her own. What do you want to happen—have your child come looking for you? Get another chance at being a *mamm* to that child in fifteen or twenty years?"

Eve had to admit that thought had crossed her mind. If her child knew that she'd loved him…would he come find her one day?

"Maybe?" she whispered.

"And what happens then? Your husband will have a rather large shock when he finds out that the girl he married had already given birth to a baby. That sort of secret has a way of rocking a marriage, my dear. From what I understood, you wanted to give this child up to another Amish family so that you could get married and have more *kinner* with a husband."

"*Yah*, that's true…" Eve sighed.

"Then do that," Lovina said. "If it's what you want, then stop feeling guilty!"

"You're really telling me that?" Eve demanded. "No guilt?"

"This child is half-English," Lovina said softly. "And you had no choice in getting pregnant. Eve, *no guilt*. That Englisher took not only your innocence, but he took your ability to live a good Amish life. This was not your choice, and if you still want that good Amish life, then I don't judge you for it. I promise you that. And this family that you're considering—Thomas and Patience Wiebe—they can't have more *kinner* of their own, and adoption is the only way for them. You'd be doing something beautiful for that family."

"I've been told that," she agreed, swallowing hard. "But the other family—they have six *kinner* already."

"Then your child would have older siblings to learn from," Lovina said. "Do you want your child to have a good, Amish upbringing?"

"*Yah.*"

"Then let go. And let the woman you choose be the *mamm* to this baby. It won't be easy, but it's better than causing a ruckus later to your own life. Sometimes love means doing the hardest thing possible."

Eve nodded. Letting go had been easier to imagine earlier in her pregnancy. When the baby was just a little poke and flutter, she could imagine letting go. But now—

"Unless you've changed your mind," Lovina said.

"Or if you're unsure about this. I'm not trying to push you in any direction. I just want to make sure you know what you're doing."

"*Daet* wants me to give this baby up," Eve said.

But what would her *mamm* have said if she'd lived? Likely the same thing, but kindlier. *Mamm* would have helped her through this. *Daet* had never been the most eloquent when it came to emotions and feelings.

"Your *daet* wants you to be as happy as possible in your life, and he's furious about the man who took the life you wanted from you. It's different than him simply wanting you to give this baby to another family."

Her father loved her as much as she loved this baby inside her, and he wanted her to have a life. But what kind of life would she give her child if she brought him home with her? She'd never marry—the competition was rather fierce when it came to landing a marriage partner, and a single mother wasn't going to win. Her child would have the stigma attached of being born outside of wedlock—but worse, being the result of that kind of trauma. No, a life with her would not be sweeter for this innocent baby.

"I've gone over this in my head a thousand times," Eve said. "My baby will have a better life with another family."

Lovina nodded. "That's a loving choice."

"I hope so."

"And I know you've been feeling unready to meet this couple, but Eve, this is not going to get easier. It might actually help to see them—to be able to imagine the kind of life your baby will have growing up. You're due in two weeks—and babies have a way of defying those due dates. You could have this child any day now."

Eve sucked in a slow breath. "Meeting them makes it feel final."

"Maybe that's what you need."

Eve was silent.

"And I don't want to put the weight of other people's expectations onto you, dear," Lovina went on, "but Thomas and Patience are on pins and needles right now. They want a baby desperately, and it isn't very often that a child arrives in Redemption in need of a family. If you don't want to give your child to them, it's kinder to just tell them. This is agony for them, too."

While Eve wanted this to be about her alone, it wasn't. In a community, everything affected everyone else. This would affect her father and her sisters at home. It would affect Thomas and Patience here in Redemption. Maybe it felt good to stay on the sidelines, hold back her firm decision and allow herself to wonder what it would be like to keep this baby, but it wasn't fair to anyone else.

Would she keep this baby? If she had to be brutally honest with herself and cut past the emotion and her own longing, then she'd have to admit that no, she wouldn't. It would hurt, but she'd give this child up because it was better for the baby, and it gave her a chance at a life, too. That Englisher had taken her innocence, but he wouldn't take the rest of her life away from her.

"I should meet them," Eve said, her voice firming.

"That's a good idea," her aunt replied.

"I'd like to see their home, actually," Eve added. "I'd

like to see where my baby would grow up if I choose them."

"Should I see if you can go to their home for dinner, then?" Lovina asked. "Set a date, make this firm? I can go see them myself, tonight."

"*Yah*. If you'd be willing to do that for me," Eve said with a quick nod. "Thank you."

Lovina leaned over and slid and arm around Eve's shoulders. "*Gott* will get you through this, too, you know."

"I know…" Eve swallowed. *Gott* was here with her, and she could still feel His presence. Her mistakes hadn't taken that away from her. She'd made a mistake, and everything had changed except for that one constant certainty—*Gott* was still by her side.

One day, she'd like to get married, and for some reason when she imagined a husband now, he was looking an awful lot like that Noah Wiebe—strong, handsome and capable of making her stomach flutter with a single look.

She pushed him out of her mind. She wasn't here to find a marriage match—she was here for a goodbye.

Chapter Four

When Noah came into Redemption Carpentry the next morning, peeling off his coat and hanging it on a hook, Thomas looked up from the lathe and turned off the gas-powered engine. Thomas grinned at him, a sparkle in his eye.

"Where is Amos?" Noah asked, glancing around.

"He went to square up his tab with Wayne at the dry goods store," Thomas replied. "It's not fair to leave it hanging, especially not at this time of year."

"*Yah*, of course," Noah agreed, and he eyed his brother. "You look cheery."

Noah headed to the woodstove that was already piping heat into both the display room and the shop, and he rubbed his hands in front of it.

"Lovina came by last night," Thomas said. "She wanted to set up a visit with Eve. Lovina said that Eve is ready to meet us, and she wanted to see our home."

"*Yah?*" Noah smiled. "That's great."

"I suggested she come for dinner tonight," Thomas said. "Patience is a nervous wreck. She started scrubbing the minute Lovina left. She wants everything to be perfect."

"Have you told Rue about it?" Noah asked.

"We didn't tell her, exactly," Thomas replied. "She overheard us talking about it, and she came bursting into our room, so overjoyed at the thought of having a baby brother or sister, and…we couldn't just lie to her, could we?"

Noah grinned at the thought of his little niece's rambunctious nature. She'd been ecstatic to have Patience as a new mother, and she'd very solemnly accepted Noah as her uncle, and it seemed her enthusiasm was going to bridge this, too.

"Wait…you were talking about it in English?" Noah asked.

"It would appear that Rue has picked up enough Dutch to know the words for new baby, mom and dad, big sister, and a few other things that let her piece it all together," Thomas said with a sigh. "I should be proud that she's learning the language so fast."

"You *are* proud of that," Noah countered with a laugh.

"Fine, I am," Thomas admitted. "But I'm also seeing the difficulty in keeping conversations private from *kinner* when you can't just speak in a language they don't understand."

Noah chuckled. Rue had arrived as a little Englisher girl who stubbornly refused all things Amish. And now, she looked the part of an Amish child, except for her hair that had bangs in the front and kept getting into her eyes. But there was still that wild, free part of Rue that would not be tamed, except, possibly, by a younger sibling.

"So she's excited, too?" Noah asked.

"Yah..." Thomas sobered. "I now have a little girl with her hopes up, too. We told her that we weren't sure what would happen, and that maybe, just maybe, Eve would pick us. But then Rue got it into her head that if we prayed for that baby, *Gott* would give it to us. And she wanted to pray right then and there, in the middle of our bed."

"Oh, dear..." Noah felt his stomach sink. "And she's only just learned about *Gott*. If this doesn't go as we hope—"

"I'm afraid of it shaking her faith," Thomas agreed. "But Patience is brilliant. She told Rue that we mustn't pray only for ourselves. We have to pray for Eve, too, and for the baby, and for *Gott* to work things out for the best for everyone."

Noah sighed. "It's tough."

"Incredibly tough," Thomas agreed. "But all the same, tonight we'll meet her over dinner. And *Gott* willing, she'll be impressed with our family and want to leave her baby with us. I don't think there was any way of introducing Eve to Rue without Rue figuring it out anyway."

"I'm sure it will go well," Noah said. "Just relax. You're a loving family. Eve will see that."

"Do you want to come?" Thomas asked.

"Me?" Noah shook his head. "Why?"

"Because you're part of this family, and she already seems to like you," Thomas said. "I think having you there might help, actually. Besides, I don't feel right keeping secrets. This baby is due very soon, and I want her to know exactly the kind of family we are—all of us, *Mamm* included. I won't feel right about it otherwise."

Noah blew out a breath. This was a delicate time, and while Thomas seemed to think this was a good idea, he didn't want to have to face Patience if Eve didn't choose them for her child… What if he said something stupid? He already seemed to talk a whole lot more than he should around that woman.

"I'll tell you what," Noah said slowly. "I'll ask Eve if she wants me there. That's probably the safest thing to do. She's the one who needs to be comfortable, right?"

"Probably wise," Thomas agreed.

The door opened again, and this time Amos came inside along with a rush of cold air and a swirl of icy snowflakes. He slammed the door shut and pulled off his gloves.

"It's cold out there!" Amos said. "I gave all the horses some extra feed. I think they'll need it." Amos rubbed a hand over his beard and looked between them. "What's going on?"

They brought him up to speed, and Amos nodded sagely.

"All right. Good!" Amos shrugged. "Thomas, this is a good thing! It looks to me like *Gott* is working in this. It's all perfect. She needs a family for her child, and you'd love nothing more than to be that family. *Gott* brought her here. Let's trust that *Gott* can finish what He started, shall we?"

"*Yah…*" Thomas said with a sigh. "I suppose part of my problem is that it's not just Patience and Rue with their hopes up. It's me, too. I'd love nothing more than to raise a baby. I didn't get to do that with Rue, and I missed out. But to start fresh—to raise a little one from a babe in arms and be the *daet* that child always knew… I'd like that."

Noah's heart gave a squeeze. Thomas didn't talk often about what he'd missed out on when Rue's Englisher mother kept him away. But it had hurt him deeply—Noah knew that much. If he could help his brother, he would. One thing was certain—this baby was going to come into this world deeply wanted by more people than could do the raising.

Noah rubbed his hand through his hair, and then reached for his hat.

"I'm going to bring some food over to Wollie's hotel room," he said.

"*Yah*, of course," Thomas replied. "Don't be too long, though. I need you to help me finish up that tall cabinet. I can't move it alone."

"I won't take too long," he promised, and he headed out into the cold street and next door to Quilts and Such. He'd promised Eve that he'd take her with him, and he found himself feeling a little thrill of anticipation at seeing her again.

Noah paused when he entered the fabric shop, and then he spotted Eve refilling a display of Amish Christmas tree decorations—tiny knitted red mittens, crocheted snowflakes and little cardboard barns that lit up on the inside with battery-operated lights.

Eve saw him at the same time and she smiled. He headed over to her. Lovina was chatting on the other side of the store with her brother-in-law, Bishop Glick, so they had some privacy for the time being.

"Are you ready to come see Wollie?" he asked.

"Yah." She nodded, then licked her lips. "My aunt and I put together a few items for them—some blankets, towels, sheets, that sort of thing. If Mary Lapp baked, we know she'll have done justice to it."

"Yah, there's a lot of food," he said with a chuckle. "Where is it? I'll carry it out—the buggy's hitched."

It didn't take long to get the buggy loaded up, and when Eve came out back to where he was waiting, she looked cheerful. He helped her up into the buggy and then got up beside her. The day was bright and sunny, and he was telling himself that his cheeriness was due to the weather, but he knew that wasn't entirely true.

"I heard that you've got plans for dinner at my brother's place tonight," he said.

Eve tugged the blanket over her lap. *"Yah.* I thought I should. My aunt pointed out that Thomas and Patience are on pins and needles waiting for my decision, so drawing this out is more painful for everyone." She raised her gaze to meet his. "Will you be there?"

"I could…if you wanted me there," he replied.

"The thing is," she said, lowering her voice further, "my aunt is connected to everyone in this town—even the bishop!"

"Yah, I know," he said with a small smile.

"Anyway, Lovina has a strong personality, and I don't want to be pushed into anything, you know? I don't think she'd mean to because she really is trying to be supportive, but if she drives me to your brother's home, there is a better than average chance that she'll stay to dinner because she's the family I have here. And—" Her cheeks flushed. "I'd rather she didn't."

"Ah, I see," Noah said. "I'm happy to drive you. I don't have to stay to dinner, either. I can just drop you off and pick you up later."

"No, you should stay," she replied, and then a smile tickled her lips. "If I want a quick exit, I'll need you."

Noah chuckled at that. "Okay... I could see that."

"I'm only halfway joking about that quick exit," she said. "Would you be offended if I asked you drive me home early...should I need it?"

"Not at all," he replied. "You're in full control of this, Eve. I promise. When you want to leave, I'll drive you. No questions asked."

"That's kind," she said.

"It's only right," he replied. "I can take you after work is done—we can go straight there, if that's okay."

Eve nodded. "*Yah*, thank you."

The hotel where the Zook family was staying was on the far end of Redemption, away from the Amish tourist section of town. It was a one-story affair with plenty of parking, and while the parking lot wasn't exactly Amish friendly, Noah knew the area well enough and parked his buggy next to a car. Eve looked around uncertainly.

"It'll be fine," Noah said. "I parked here last time. We won't stay long anyway."

He put his horses' feed bags on before helping Eve down onto the salted driveway.

"When did you see Wollie last?" she asked.

"I dropped off some food earlier this week," he said, then he headed around to the back of the buggy and pulled out the covered basket that contained *Mammi*'s baking—whoopee pies, cinnamon buns, cookies...even a chocolate pie. He was about to grab the plastic bag containing the linens Lovina was sending, but he looked over at Eve, standing there in the patchy snow.

"I'll come back for it," he said, and he offered her his arm.

Eve put her hand into the crook of his arm, and he found that he liked the way this felt—being the strong arm for a woman to depend on...and maybe even for this particular woman. He led the way to the last room at the far end of the strip. That was where the Zooks were staying, but before he knocked, he glanced down at her. Eve was looking determinedly at the door, her jaw tense and her cheeks pale.

When Noah knocked, the door opened a moment later revealing Wollie dressed in jeans, a long-sleeved shirt, and sock feet. Wollie looked between them, his face registering shock, and it was only when Noah saw his friend's bewildered expression that he realized how this looked.

"Noah...and Eve?" Wollie laughed, and then bent down to give his cousin a brief hug. "I had no idea! Noah, you've kept a rather good secret, my friend!"

And for just a single moment, Noah felt what it would be like to introduce a wife to an old friend...and it felt better than it should.

"No, no—" Eve's pallor suddenly turned pink. "We're not—it's not—" She looked up at Noah. "Maybe you go get that linen?"

Right—she'd need some privacy for explanations. He should have thought of that. He handed Wollie the basket of food with a rueful smile and wordlessly headed back toward the buggy. He took his time about gathering up the cloth bags that Lovina had set out for the

Zooks, and when he returned to the hotel room, the explanations seemed to be out of the way, because both Wollie and his wife were looking at Eve with sympathy in their eyes.

"I'm back," he said, carrying in the last of the bags.

"It's good to see you again," Wollie said, coming over to shake his hand. "And thank you for bringing my cousin. It's been…eight or nine years?"

"Something like that," Eve agreed. "You look the same… I mean, English, but…"

Noah knew what she meant. Wollie still had a certain Amish quality about him, no matter what an Englisher barber did to his hair, or what clothes he wore.

The hotel room was cramped for a family with four children. There were two queen-size beds, a TV playing in one corner, and not much else. Wollie's wife, Natasha, had her toddler daughter on her hip, but the little girl's fingers were in her mouth and her attention was locked on the television that a brother and sister were watching from one of the beds. The older boy, who looked about eight, stood next to his mother, watching them curiously.

"I'm Noah. I'm one of your *daet*'s friends," Noah said. "And you've met Eve? She's your…"

"She's my cousin," Wollie said with a smile. "And Noah's a friend from a really long time ago. We played together when we were your age, Caleb."

"Wow." Caleb looked properly impressed, and he stuck out his hand and Noah shook it. It looked like Wollie was raising his *kinner* with some Amish manners—that was nice to see.

"Do you like whoopee pies?" Noah asked.

"Yeah!" The boy grinned, and Noah couldn't help but smile at the fact that this English boy loved Amish desserts. "Well, we've got whoopee pies and more in that basket over there. We hope it makes things a little cheerier."

"Thank you for this," Natasha said. "We do appreciate it. You've all been really wonderful."

"We're putting together as much as we can," Noah assured them. "And in January, my brother and I will give you some bedroom furniture of your choice, too."

"That's too much," Wollie said, his voice firming. "I know how much you sell your work for, and that's a hit to your bottom line. I've got insurance to cover that."

"We're still here for you," Noah replied. "And you know there's a place for you if you come back to the Amish life."

Wollie and Natasha exchanged a look, and she slipped away, carrying the basket to the bed for the kids to come look through. Eve followed her and sank on the edge of the bed. She glanced over her shoulder once toward the men.

"And if we don't come back?" Wollie asked, switching to Dutch for privacy. "For Natasha—it's not what she was raised to do, you know."

"We heard that you might want to," Noah said.

"Wanting to do something and having the ability to make it work—" Wollie shook his head. "Natasha isn't Amish. I knew that when I married her. I can't push this."

"Whatever you decide to do, we're providing you with bedroom furniture," Noah said firmly. "I'm standing by it."

Wollie's face colored and he nodded. "You're a good man, Noah. I may have spoken too enthusiastically when I saw my parents last."

Looking around that hotel room at the Zook family, he could see exactly why it would be complicated. These *kinner* weren't Amish, and neither was their mother. Natasha looked even more English next to Eve's somber clothing and neat *kapp* in her hair.

"And my cousin?" Wollie asked, lowering his voice further. "Is she going to be okay?"

"*Yah*, I think so," Noah replied. "Did she tell you why she's here?"

"To have the baby and…give it up?" Wollie asked sadly.

Noah nodded. *"Yah."*

"Natasha and I aren't in a position to take in another child," he said.

"I don't think she's here for that," Noah said. "She cares about you and wanted to make this time here about something more than…the baby."

Wollie met Noah's gaze. "She was a sweet kid— smart, kind. I really liked her."

"I think she felt the same way about you," Noah replied. "From what she's told me."

"She's Amish—I probably won't see much of her," Wollie said. "You'll look out for her, won't you?"

"For as long as she's here," Noah agreed. "Of course."

"Thank you." Wollie pressed his lips together. "I appreciate that."

And here Noah and Eve were trying to do the same for Wollie. He was more part of their Amish community than he thought, even now. This was what community was for—for the hard and worrying times.

"How are you doing otherwise?" Noah asked.

"I've still got a job," Wollie said. "And the insurance agent is getting things cleared away so we can get some money to restart. It'll be okay."

"I'm glad to hear that," Noah said. "And your parents?"

"They're fine." Wollie smiled weakly. "Still deeply disappointed in me, but fine."

"*Yah*, well… Amish parents, right?" Noah said—it was an old joke, and Wollie chuckled, too.

"Amish parents…" he agreed. "Funny. I always thought I'd end up being an Amish *daet* one day. Didn't turn out that way."

"You're more Amish than you think, Wollie," Noah replied.

"I've actually got to get to work soon," Wollie said. "My shift starts in about an hour."

"We'd best get back, too," Noah said. "But just to let you know, we're collecting household items for you—the whole town is pitching in, and we'll get you back onto your feet. That's a promise."

"Like I said, I have insurance," Wollie said.

"You also have us."

"I do appreciate it, Noah." Wollie shook his hand firmly, and his eyes misted. "You're a good friend. Just make sure my cousin is taken care of, too."

"You can count on it," Noah said.

They said their goodbyes, Eve gave Natasha a smile and a nod, and then they headed back out to where the buggy was waiting. But something from this visit had stuck in Noah's heart. Wollie had a family—and seeing that family struck home how much a man changed with marriage and *kinner*. This wasn't Wollie's choice to come back—it would have to be a family decision…like his own parents had made. His parents had taken on the challenge of joining the Amish life together. For all the things that frustrated him about his mother, Rachel Wiebe was a brave woman to do it.

It was very likely too much to hope that Wollie and Natasha could do the same.

"What did you think of his wife?" Noah asked as he flicked the reins and they headed back out to the street once more.

"She's nice," Eve said. "I can see why he loves her."

Noah looked over at Eve and smiled faintly. *Yah*, a man could fall in love with the right woman rather easily. But making a life with her wasn't always so simple.

Wollie went English for a very nice woman, and he may very well have to stay that way.

Chapter Five

That evening after the sun had set, leaving the town of Redemption aglow with streetlights that reflected cheerily off the Christmas decorations, Lovina flicked the sign to Closed and locked the door. The fire in the pot-bellied stove had burned down, and Eve pulled on her uncle's heavy coat, wrapping it around herself.

"The sales were very good today," Lovina said, opening the till. She pulled out the first batch of bills and began to count them, her lips moving silently as she worked.

"*Yah*, it looks that way." Eve perched on the edge of a stool, watching her aunt flick through the stacks of bills.

"Are you sure you don't want me to come with you tonight?" Lovina asked, pausing in her counting. "I'd be happy to offer moral support. This is a difficult time, I know, and I'd just feel better knowing that I was there for you. I think your father would feel better, too."

"I appreciate it," Eve replied. "And you have been wonderful, Aunty. I just think it's better if I see their home alone. I have to be able to look back on this later and feel confident in my choice, and that will be easier to do if I go by myself."

Lovina nodded and made a note on a bank deposit form, and moved on to the next pile of bills. "I do understand that, dear. This is an incredibly personal choice."

"Do you have any advice, though?" Eve asked. "Anything I should be looking for?"

Lovina was silent for a moment, her brow furrowed.

"Just pray for *Gott*'s guidance," Lovina said. "And... maybe expect to feel some conflicting emotions when you meet Patience."

"Is there something off-putting about her?" Eve asked, straightening. "Anything I should know?"

"Nothing." Lovina made another note on the bank slip, wrapped it around the bills, slipped the money into a plastic bank bag and sealed it. "It's just... I'm only thinking about how I might feel in your situation, and I imagine it would be hard to meet the woman who might be your baby's *mamm*. There would be some very natural feelings attached to that... Some jealousy, maybe. Some protectiveness."

That was sage advice, Eve had to admit. She wasn't looking forward to seeing Patience. She would be a lovely woman, no doubt, but even the thought of seeing her had Eve's stomach in knots.

There was a tap on the front door, and Eve turned to see Noah through the window.

"He's here," Lovina said with a reassuring smile. "It will be okay. I know it."

Eve exchanged a look with her aunt, then she rose to her feet. There was no use putting this off—if she was looking for a family for her baby, she'd just found a very good match. So why didn't she feel more peace about this?

"I'll be praying for you," Lovina said. "And I'll wait up for you." Lovina gave her a nod.

There was something reassuring about having someone wait up for her, and Eve said a silent prayer for guidance this evening. She needed to know, beyond any shadow of doubt, that she was making the right choice.

Eve and Noah headed back out into the street, pulled the door shut behind them, and when Eve looked in through the window, she saw her aunt's troubled gaze following her. Was Lovina uncertain about this choice in family, or was her concern something deeper?

But it wasn't Lovina's concern that should be influencing her tonight—tonight was about meeting a family without the benefit of her aunt's opinions to steer her.

Noah had the buggy ready to go, the horses stamping impatiently in the icy snow.

"Let me help you," Noah said, and Eve pulled herself out of her thoughts. She accepted his hand and hoisted herself up into the buggy.

There were two folded blankets on the seat, and while Noah got into the buggy next to her, she arranged the blankets over her legs. He flicked the reins and the horses started forward, the wheels crunching over the packed snow.

The few Englisher businesses along this street had Christmas lights circling their windows, and the streetlights had large green wreaths with shining red berries. The sky was clear, but the stars weren't visible here in town—just the silvery moon that hung low in the sky.

That morning, Eve had been reading the Christmas

story in her Bible. It was a solitary feeling to be carrying a child without a husband to support her, or a community to celebrate this baby. In years past, Eve hadn't appreciated how difficult Jesus's birth would have been for Mary. In Bible stories, Mary seemed different from people today—holier, stronger, braver. But now, pregnant with her own child outside of her society's approved boundaries, Eve wondered how frightened Mary might have been. Because Eve was terrified.

"You know, Wollie asked me to look out for you today," Noah said.

"Did he?" She smiled at that. "He always was a nice, older cousin."

And neither of them had ended up with the proper Amish life, had they? She might be determined to stay Amish, but she had a hard road ahead of her.

"He's worried about you, I think," Noah said.

"Well, I'm equally worried about him," she replied frankly. "I still have a chance at an Amish life. I'm not sure he does."

"*Gott* knows," Noah said.

"*Yah...*" Only *Gott* knew what was in store for any of them, and there were some problems that only *Gott* could fix.

"My brother is so excited to meet you," Noah said.

They came to the end of Main Street and turned onto a smaller road, past Englisher houses with front yards covered in children's boot prints, windows lit from within and Christmas trees sparkling.

"*Yah?*" she said faintly.

"He could talk about nothing else all afternoon," Noah said. When she didn't answer, he added, "I know this is a hopeful evening for my brother, but for you—I imagine it's different."

"Yah," she admitted. "I hate this—every step of it. But we can't refuse to do what we have to, can we?"

"I'm sorry," he said. "I wish I could make it easier somehow."

"I don't think you can," she said. "I'm doing this for a reason, though. That Englisher boy took away more than he ever knew, I'm sure. He took away my ability to have a proper, Amish life. I want a husband and a houseful of my own *kinner.* The truly sad thing is that I want what your brother and his wife want—I just can't have it yet. I want to cook breakfast for my own family. I want a husband to drive me to church, and I want all the trials and challenges that come with raising and loving a large family. I've always wanted that."

"And your chance at that beautiful life was taken from you," he said.

"Yah. Without my consent. Against my will." She sucked in a deep breath. "If I'd had a boyfriend, and I'd made the mistake, I might be less angry. But I didn't! I was in the wrong place at the wrong time! That Englisher destroyed *my life.*" Her voice trembled. "Is it fair to ask me to give up the rest of my life because of something I didn't choose?"

"I agree," he said quietly. "You don't deserve this."

"My *daet*… If you'd seen his face." Eve sighed. "He wanted more for me. If I stay single, and never get married, I'll be his responsibility to care for. I'll stay a dependant. I'll likely be a hindrance to him remarrying one day."

"I'm sure your *daet* doesn't see it that way," Noah countered.

"But I do."

She hadn't sat by her mother's bedside, listening to her last bits of advice, for nothing. Eve wanted to be a good daughter, and eventually, a good wife. She wanted to live out her beliefs with her Amish community, and she wanted to pass down her love for *Gott* to her own *kinner.*

Rebellion isn't worth it, her *mamm* had told her. *Be a good girl, and you'll reap the rewards of having made solid choices. Going a little wild might feel good in the moment, but there is only regret at the end of that road. Trust me, my dear girl.*

And Eve had promised *Gott* that she'd follow her *mamm*'s advice. She'd stay to the narrow path, and she'd embrace all of *Gott*'s best that He had waiting for her.

For it to be taken from her like that? To have a child out of wedlock and become completely unmarriageable, all because of one despicable Englisher who tricked her? Could she lose *Gott*'s best for her just as easily as that?

"My *mamm* told me stories about girls who made unwise choices," Eve said. "She even told me about Wollie—how he went English and all he'd given up for an Englisher girl. She didn't want me to do the same thing—fall in love with an Englisher and have no path home again." Eve sucked in a breath of frigid air. "Maybe *Gott*'s best for me will have to change, too, now."

"I don't have the answers," Noah said quietly. "Maybe the bishop has more than I do, but I just can't imagine that we're powerful enough to thwart *Gott*'s plans. *Gott* is still working, Eve. He has to be."

Eve fell silent for a few beats, mulling over his words. But she'd had enough of talking of her own sadness.

"Tell me about your niece," Eve said instead.

Noah looked over at her uncertainly.

"Please," she added. "I'd like to hear about her."

For the rest of the ride, Noah chatted on about his little niece, whom he seemed very attached to. It was good to see that the girl in that home was surrounded by a devoted extended family. If her child joined them, her half-Englisher baby would be equally loved.

Would Thomas and Patience's home be enough to give *this* child a reason to stay Amish, too?

Chapter Six

Eve sucked in a wavering breath as Noah steered the horses into a driveway and they plodded toward a little one-story house. This was an acreage, obviously, and she could make out a stable in the darkness, illuminated by the light coming from Noah's headlamps. The house looked snug, and it glowed cozily into the frigid night. Her stomach clenched in nervousness, as Noah reined in the horses in front of the house, and she felt his hand touch her sleeve.

"You okay?" Noah asked, his voice low.

"Uh—" She tried to force a smile but wasn't sure it was successful. "I'll have to be."

"They're very nice people," he said.

The door opened, and a young man appeared in the doorway. He had a short russet-colored beard and a kind face. She could see the family resemblance between the two men, so this must be Thomas. He pulled on a coat as he stepped outside, and dropped a hat onto his head. He came out onto the steps with a nervous smile.

"Hello!" he said. "Noah, I'll help you with the horses."

"*Yah*, thanks," Noah replied, and he looked over at Eve again, and lowered his voice. "They're very nice. I promise."

A woman appeared in the doorway behind Thomas, and a little girl who was only barely being restrained.

"Is it her?" the girl asked, a little too loudly in English.

The woman bent to talk to her, and Noah hopped to the ground. He held out his hand, and then stepped closer to help her descend. She managed to get down with a little more dignity than the last time he'd helped her out of a buggy, and she glanced up to see Thomas Weibe looking at her hopefully. He put out a hand.

"It's a pleasure to meet you," Thomas said.

Eve shook his hand, and Thomas gestured behind him. "That is my wife, Patience, and our daughter, Rue. If you want to go in where it's warm, Noah and I will join you in a few minutes."

"*Yah*, I'll do that," Eve said, and with one last glance at Noah, whose gaze was locked on her almost protectively, she headed toward the open door.

"Come in," Patience said as Eve came up the steps. "You must be freezing. I have tea on, if you want some."

Eve came into the house, the welcome warmth enveloping her. She slid off her coat and Patience hung it up for her with a smile.

"My name is Patience," she said, and the introductions were made.

After having said a polite hello, Eve glanced around the entryway. It wasn't quite a full mudroom—but it did give some space from the kitchen, which she could see directly into from where she stood. A big, black stove dominated one side of the room, and a bank of tall white cupboards flanked the other side. The floor was a polished dark wood, and the solid kitchen table was the same color as the floor.

An older woman sat at the kitchen table. She had graying hair and a neat dress. She stood up as Eve came in and gave her a smile. Who was this, in the family circle?

"This is my mother-in-law," Patience said.

Noah and Thomas's mother...it was nice to see her, actually. This would be her child's grandmother if Eve chose the Wiebe family.

"It's nice to meet you. I'm Rachel," the older woman said. "Come, sit down. Do you want some cookies? I'm just going to get the pot of tea ready."

"No, I'm not hungry," Eve said, and she felt heat rise in her cheeks. "I mean—" She was there for dinner, after all.

"You're nervous, too," Patience said.

"Yah," she admitted with a shaky smile. "I am."

"I think we all are," Patience replied.

"What are you saying?" Rue whispered to Patience.

"This is Rue," Patience said, switching to English. "She doesn't understand very much Dutch, but she's learning, aren't you, sugar?"

"Yah, I'm learning," Rue said proudly. "I can ask for the bathroom in Dutch. Do you want to hear it?"

The women laughed, and Patience smoothed a hand over the girl's straight blond hair.

"Not just now," Patience said gently.

Eve sank down into a kitchen chair; the little girl sat down next to her and put a hand on the side of her belly.

"Rue, you can't just—" Patience started.

"It's okay," Eve said. In a way, it was nice to have someone, even a very young someone, react to her pregnant form with some spontaneous happiness. "Can you feel that? That's the baby moving."

"I can feel it!" Rue's eyes lit up. "Is that my baby brother or sister?"

Eve hesitated, meeting the little girl's expectant gaze. Rue's breath was bated, and her little hand rested on Eve's stomach hopefully. Even this little girl was hoping for this baby…and that was almost heartbreaking.

"We talked about this, Rue," Patience said. "We don't know yet. We have to ask *Gott* to do what's best for all of us, and we don't know what that answer is yet."

What was best for all of them… That was a tall order that Eve wasn't even sure could be answered this side of glory.

"I'm sorry," Patience said, switching into Dutch again. "She's very young, and she overheard us talking. Apparently, she understands more Dutch than we gave her credit for. We would have tried to be more discreet. Please don't take this as pressure from us."

"No, of course not," Eve replied.

Such polite discussion over the future of her unborn baby…

"Have some tea?" Rachel asked, coming back to the table with a teapot. She put it on top of a cork pot holder, and then headed back to the counter for teacups.

"Thank you," Eve said. It was something to do with her hands, at least.

"Patience here is a wonderful teacher," Rachel said, returning with a teetering pile of cups. "She's not teaching at the schoolhouse anymore—she just finished the semester—but there are a few boys that come by for some extra help with their reading after school. She's got a real gift with *kinner.*"

"Oh?" Eve said.

Rachel poured Eve a cup of tea and nudged a sugar bowl toward her.

"This home is a loving, supportive home for a child who is half-English," Rachel said in Dutch. "Rue has come such a long way in a short period of time. Her Englisher mother had bought her all sorts of clothes that weren't appropriate for an Amish girl to wear, and as you can imagine, it was very difficult for Rue to let go. She'd lost her mother, and those clothes were a connection to her."

"Poor thing," Eve murmured, looking down at Rue, who now had her elbows planted on the table.

"Yah..." Rachel agreed. "But Patience was the one who had the idea to turn that Englisher clothing into a quilt for her, and Rue sleeps with it every night now."

"Are you talking about my quilt?" Rue piped up.

"See? She understands more Dutch than we think!" Rachel chuckled.

"My *mammi* is teaching me to talk like everyone else," Rue said soberly. "And that's because she was born regular, just like me."

"Regular?" Eve asked weakly.

"She means English," Rachel replied, some color coming into her cheeks. "I was born English, and my husband and I converted when our *kinner* were very young."

This was information that hit Eve like a wet slap.

Eve gave Rachel a second look. Come to think of it, the older woman did lack a few of those Amish facial characteristics.

"And *Mammi* even went back to live regular for a while, too!" Rue added with a bright smile. "But then she came back again."

"About the same time that Rue arrived, actually," Rachel said uncomfortably. "I apologize, Eve. This wasn't quite how I intended to tell you about my history."

"Were you going to tell me at all?" Eve asked, her voice tight. Because up until now, there had been plenty of opportunity for both Lovina and Noah to fill her in, and neither of them had said a word.

"Yes, I was going to tell you," Rachel said. "Of course! Why do you think I'm here tonight? We aren't the kind of people who ask to adopt a baby without giving all the information."

Englishers… The very thought made her stomach turn and her heart speed up. She'd had very limited contact with the Englishers in her life. Wollie going English had been a shock to the entire family—one so terrible that they only talked about it away from other people. She'd never worked at a store or dealt with tourists directly until she'd come to Redemption, but she had discovered what kind of people the English were at that party nine months ago. And this woman—Thomas's own *mamm*—was English born, and had even reverted to English ways rather recently. She could hear her own heartbeat thudding inside her skull.

"I can see that this has been a shock," Rachel said softly. "And I'm very sorry about this. You see, I thought it might help if you met me directly, if you could see that I'm no different from you—"

"But you *are* different from me," Eve said, and Rachel recoiled.

"Am I?" Rachel asked. "If I hadn't said anything, would you have guessed?"

"The English are different from us. They're raised differently. They see the world differently! They see *Gott* differently!"

"We aren't a different species," Rachel replied. "We're all human. And I'm as Amish as you—I was baptized into the church, and I raised my *kinner* in the faith, too."

"*Yah*, all human," Eve agreed. "But you aren't as Amish as me. You were raised with different expectations in behavior and in…everything. I was raised to want *Gott*'s way and to be satisfied with my role. Were you?"

"I was raised Mennonite," Rachel said tersely. "I didn't exactly come off the bottom of someone's shoe. And I've loved *Gott* all my life. You can't assume that because I wasn't born on one of these farms that I didn't know *Gott*. Is He so narrow that He can only be found here?"

"So you're saying that the Amish life isn't necessary?" Eve asked. "It's all the same—Amish, English…"

"No!" Patience interjected for the first time, and her face flushed red. The room fell silent, and even little Rue stared up at Patience in shock. "No, she isn't saying that!" Patience closed her eyes, and then lowered her voice. "The Amish life matters—and we are a devoted Amish family. Our faith, our way of life, our language—it's what makes us who we are and draws us closer together as a community and closer to *Gott*. No one here is suggesting that there is no difference."

Tears rose in Rachel's eyes, and she looked toward her daughter-in-law, stricken. "I didn't mean that," Rachel said, and then turned to Eve. "It's just…sometimes when you weren't born in the Amish faith, you get treated differently when people find out. People can act like you're lower, almost. I just mean that on a human level, we're the same. It's our choices that matter, that change us. I didn't mean to get testy. I was just being overly sensitive. I'm sorry."

Rachel's Dutch was flawless. If she hadn't told Eve, she wouldn't have guessed…and that scared her, too. Because this family was offering her child an Englisher grandmother.

Even if that Englisher grandmother spoke excellent Dutch.

The door opened just then and the men came back inside. They pulled off their boots and washed their hands, then came into the kitchen. Thomas hesitated, looking around the room.

"I'm hungry," he said, a little too cheerfully.

Noah met Eve's gaze, and he winced. Did he guess at what she'd just discovered?

"We were—uh—just discussing your mother's history," Patience said weakly.

"Oh…" Thomas nodded. "We wanted my *mamm* to be here so that you could meet her properly."

"*Yah*, she mentioned that," Eve replied.

Patience and Rachel exchanged a look, and Eve noticed the silent apology passing between them. Rachel might have been born English, and even returned to her English life for a while, but she was a part of this family.

Noah came into the kitchen and when Thomas gestured for him to have a seat at the table, he pulled out a chair next to Rue and sat down. Noah glanced around the table, then his warm gaze landed on Eve. His eyebrow flicked up, and she sensed the question. She smiled faintly in response. She was fine—she wasn't leaving yet.

"Since this is out now," Eve said, "I have some questions. Rachel, why did you leave the Amish life after converting? If you chose the Amish way, what made you leave again?"

Rachel looked uncomfortably toward Thomas and Patience.

"You'd best just talk about it," Thomas said. "We're here to be honest, aren't we?"

"I lost my husband," Rachel replied quietly. "And it was a difficult time for me. I missed my family— my sister, mostly. I missed who I used to be."

"Englisher, you mean," Eve said.

"No, I missed being young," Rachel said. "You won't understand that at your age. But when I lost my husband, I was suddenly a different person than I was with him. Marriage does that—it changes you fundamentally, especially the longer you're together. And when he died, I missed who I was when I was a young woman, before I'd married and had *kinner.* And having lost my husband, I had to discover who I was again—on my own."

"And who were you?" Eve asked warily.

"Me, just lonelier." Rachel dropped her gaze. "I thought I could find some part of myself that I'd laid aside, and it turned out that I couldn't. I found the old Mennonite church very comforting, and I'd missed my sister desperately. I didn't want to have to marry again to keep myself as I would with the Amish, so I got a job. I was a janitor at a school, actually. And for a little while I worked at a retail store, and then I got a job at the company my sister works for, in the mail room..." She smiled faintly. "You don't care about that, though, do you?"

"But you came back..." Eve said.

"*Yah*. The Amish life isn't an easy one, but it's the right one for me. It turns out that I had changed too much during my marriage to be able to fully embrace an English life again."

"How long were you gone?" Eve asked.

"Nearly ten years," Rachel replied. "I know that sounds terrible, but I did visit every month, and I wrote my sons letters in between those visits."

"What took so long?" Eve asked.

Rachel lifted her shoulders. "It was a process to find myself again and to come full circle. But now that I'm here, I'm here to stay."

"And what will keep my little one Amish, if this family has so many connections to the English?" Eve asked.

The room was silent for a moment, and Eve looked around at them daringly. What did they think they could give her child, with all of this rebellion in their own ranks? Was the other family better, perhaps? The solidly Amish family that would accept another child without having longed for it? Maybe so.

"We'd give your baby love," Patience said, breaking the silence. "We'd love your baby with all our hearts.

And we are an Amish family—we just aren't hiding anything from you. We're being open and honest with you because we don't believe that *Gott* can bless anything less."

"What other English family members do you have?" Eve asked.

"None we have much contact with," Thomas replied. "My mother's siblings come by once every few years, but we don't keep up with them much. It's just how things worked out."

"And Rue's family?" Eve pressed.

"Her mother was all she had," Thomas replied. "Rue's *mamm* had a tragic life of her own, and she grew up in the foster system. So there wasn't any other family to try to gain custody of her."

Eve let out a shaky breath, and she instinctively put her hand across her belly protectively. This baby was already coming from tragedy...

"I want this child raised Amish," she said. "And I don't want him or her to even know that they have any English family."

"We don't have to tell the child about—" Thomas paused, licked his lips "—about your difficulties. We could simply say that you wanted him or her to have the best life possible, and you weren't able to provide that."

And she did want her child to have the happiest, most fulfilling, most secure Amish life available—that was why Eve was here. She wanted her child to grow up happy, loved and unapologetically Amish. She wanted her child to be free from any stigma attached from a single mother.

"Why don't we eat?" Noah said, speaking for the

first time. "I don't know about all of you, but I feel better with food in my stomach. We've all been working all day."

"Yes, good idea," Patience said. "The food is ready, so let's get it onto the table."

Eve instinctively started to stand up to lend a hand in the kitchen, and Patience waved her off.

"No, Eve, sit. Be comfortable. I've never been pregnant myself, but I've seen enough pregnancies with my sisters and my friends to know that these last weeks aren't an easy time. Dinner won't take a minute."

And Eve sank back down into her chair and looked over at Noah. Rue had come up with a carved rooster and was making it walk up Noah's arm. He looked over the top of Rue's head and smiled faintly.

This was the Wiebe family—a husband who'd had an Englisher child out of wedlock, a grandmother who was Englisher born and had only recently returned, and a little half-English girl who seemed to relay all of the family secrets when she chattered.

Her child's birth story wouldn't remain a secret long in this home; she could already tell. And here, it seemed, being English wasn't something to be ashamed of.

Was that a good thing, or a bad thing? She wasn't so sure. Because in her experience, the English were not to be trusted.

"Cookie?" Noah murmured, nudging a plate toward her.

There were shortbread cookies on the plate, all in the shape of little trees. She accepted one and took a bite. It was buttery and perfectly baked.

Patience came to the table with a platter of roast beef,

and she put it down with a smile. She was pretty, slim and seemed very loving to the family around her… She was the perfect Amish mother. Or was she? What else was this family hiding?

And yet, if Eve had met Patience under different circumstances, she would have liked her. Eve watched Patience as she brought the food to the table. Thomas gave his wife an encouraging smile, and there was a tenderness between the couple that Eve couldn't help but envy. What would it be like to have a man love her the way Thomas loved Patience? It was wrong to envy, she knew that, but she couldn't help the pang all the same. One day, hopefully soon, Eve wanted this very scene for herself—a husband, a family, *kinner* that she could proudly claim as hers… Patience Wiebe was the wife and *mamm* that Eve longed to be.

For all appearances, at least.

The baby wriggled inside her, and Eve ran her hand over her stomach, feeling the baby settle at her touch. Could Eve pass the baby into this lovely woman's arms and let her be the *mumm*? Could she trust them?

The problem was, now that she'd met her, Patience was no longer an ideal to be jealous of. She was a very real woman who wouldn't be perfect…and that might be even harder to accept.

Noah sat across from his mother, and her gaze flickered toward him. There was red in her cheeks—she was embarrassed. Somehow that stabbed at his heart worse than anything else. His *mamm* might have wronged him, and he might have his own issues with her, but seeing her embarrassed…

Mamm pushed her chair back, then left the table, heading into the kitchen. Noah swallowed against the tightness in his throat. This was their family—and their private problems. He knew it was only right to be open with Eve about all of it, but it still felt like an invasion.

And yet seeing his mother's back to them, pretending to arrange buns in a bowl, but taking far too long to accomplish the task, he felt his chest constrict in sympathy. She was still his *mamm*, and she'd been hopeful that she could help in this adoption process...

Beside him, Eve nibbled at the food on her plate, as she listened to Thomas tell a story about Rue. What did Eve think of them now?

Noah pushed his chair out and stood up. He angled around the table and headed over to where his *mamm* stood by the bowl of dinner rolls.

"Mamm?" he said quietly.

She wiped her eyes hurriedly. "Yes, son?"

"Are you crying?" he asked hesitantly.

"No." But the tears in her eyes said otherwise, and he stood there awkwardly, unsure of what to do.

"Mamm, all you could be was honest," he said, putting a hand on her arm.

Rachel sucked in a breath and checked her hair with her hands.

"It's what you told me and Thomas over and over again when we were *kinner*—after we made a mistake, we had to confess and be honest."

"That wasn't a confession," *Mamm* said softly. "That was judgment."

"She doesn't know us..." Noah said. "And we're asking her to choose us—"

"I'm being judged by an unwed mother," Rachel said, and her lips wobbled.

"You were right to tell her the truth," Noah said. "I think it was…brave of you, actually. You're doing all of this to help Thomas, and I know he appreciates that."

"You didn't hear the way she spoke to me…" Rachel licked her lips. "She thinks I'm beneath her—"

"She's terrified of Englishers," Noah said. "She was taken advantage of by some Englisher boys—that's how the baby was conceived. It wasn't by choice on her part."

Rachel blinked, then darted a look back at the table. "What?"

"That pregnancy isn't her fault, and I dare say that her reaction was based on those fears," Noah replied.

Rachel nodded. "That does change things. The poor girl…"

"Yah." Noah swallowed. "I'm sure that's private information, though. And she never wants her child to know it."

"I can understand that," Rachel said, and she shook her head slowly.

"Are you okay, *Mamm*?" Noah asked.

Rachel turned toward him and gave him a nod. "I'll be fine, son. Tonight isn't about me—or it shouldn't be. Anyway, let's try to make your brother look good."

At the table, Rue was up on her knees and Thomas told her to sit down properly. Patience sat faced away from them, but from the set of her shoulders, Noah could see her tension. He knew what Thomas had been hoping for from this evening—a chance to put Eve at ease and show her they were a loving family—but Eve seemed just as tense as Patience was. She'd stopped pretending to eat, and the fork lay on her plate.

Mamm returned to the table ahead of Noah with the bowl of rolls in her hands, and Noah followed. This Christmas, they were all hoping for a special gift… a tiny bundle of joy. But that gift would come with a price for Eve, and only now was Noah realizing how steep it would be.

Rue left the table, carrying her plate to the sink, and Noah took his niece's chair next to Eve. For the next few minutes everyone talked, pretending that this was just a normal dinner.

"And how was work today, Noah?" *Mamm* asked.

"Uh—" Noah shifted uncomfortably. "It was busy."

"Did you finish that sleigh bed you were working on?" *Mamm* pressed brightly.

"No, not yet."

"Oh…"

The conversation seemed to be at a lull, and Noah felt a touch on his knee under the table. He looked over to see Eve's gaze flicker toward him, her cheeks flushed.

"I'm actually getting tired," Eve said quietly.

The table fell silent.

"Right," Noah said. "I can give you a ride home, if that's what you want."

"Please."

"I'll just go hitch up," Noah said, and he scraped his chair back and headed for the door. This was what he'd promised her he'd do…even though they hadn't succeeded yet in showing Eve the family they wanted her to see—the family they *were* beneath all the mistakes.

All the same, he didn't think Eve's decision was

going to come down to how united and happy the Wiebe family appeared to be over a dinner. It might not even come down to Rachel and her past mistakes. This decision was going to be made by Eve's personal accounting of things…and even Noah wasn't sure how that would turn out.

The question that hung almost palpably in the air was, *What does she think of us now?*

When Noah got the buggy hitched up, he brought it around to the side of the house. The door opened and Eve came out.

"Good night!" Patience called.

"If you need anything at all—" Thomas began, but he didn't finish the offer, the words hanging in the air with the cloud of his breath.

"Thank you." Eve turned toward Thomas and Patience. "I appreciate it. Good night."

Noah got down and helped her up into the buggy. Once they were both settled in, away from the winter wind, he flicked the reins and they started off. Noah looked back to see his brother standing in the doorway, his hands limp at his sides. They'd failed—Noah could feel it, too.

The evening was clear and bright, the stars twinkling overhead and the moon spilling silvery light over snow-cloaked fields. The snow seemed to absorb the sound around them as the horses plodded forward, their tack jingling in the icy air.

"They seem nice," Eve said after a couple of minutes of silence.

Noah looked over at her uncertainly. "Did you think so? You didn't seem comfortable."

"It isn't a matter of liking people," Eve replied. "This is a different kind of decision, isn't it?"

"*Yah*, you're right," he agreed.

"I was wondering about your *mamm*," she said.

Noah nodded. "I thought you might want to know more about her."

"They converted to our lifestyle?" she asked.

"*Yah*. My parents were both Mennonite, and my *daet* was working on a book about Amish life. He stayed with a bishop and his wife in a nearby community, and then *Mamm* joined him there. I guess they fell in love with our ways. The bishop in that district had some connections here in Redemption, so when my *mamm* and *daet* decided to convert, and once they understood the ways well enough, they settled into the community here. But no one really knew them from their Englisher days, so their secret was safe, for the most part."

"They came to Redemption for a fresh start," she said.

"I guess. I never knew about it growing up. I was a toddler at the time, and my brother was just a baby. They raised us as if we'd been born Amish, and we never knew any different."

"When did you find out?" she asked.

"When *Daet* died," he said, and his throat tightened. "*Mamm* told us then. It was a huge shock. We hadn't even met any of the Englisher family at that point. We knew we had some, but we also knew they thought we were crazy for living like we did, so we had nothing to do with them. My grandparents were dead. In fact, I honestly thought the bishop and his wife in the other district were our relatives until *Daet* died and *Mamm* told us differently…it was a lot to take in."

"Then your *mamm* left you?" Eve asked.

"She asked us to go with her," he replied. "She asked us to leave the Amish life behind and go back to the life she'd had before. She said she could get a job and take care of us. And we refused."

"Were you angry?" Eve whispered.

"Furious," he replied. "We'd been lied to all our lives, and then asked to leave everything we believed in behind. I was angry at *Daet* for dying, and I was angry at *Gott* for allowing it to happen. But mostly, I was angry at *Mamm* for not being strong enough. She raised us to choose the right path, no matter how hard it might be. But she didn't do that, did she? *Daet* died, and she gave up."

"Did you ever go see her life—the English one?" she asked.

"Not me. My brother did. But I didn't want to see it. She came to visit once a month, but it wasn't enough. I remember being a big, strong, teenage boy and crying alone in my bed at night because I missed my *mamm*." He laughed uncomfortably. "That's probably more than I should admit to—"

Eve slid her hand into his, and he looked down at her.

"That would have been terrible," she said. "In a way, you lost both your parents."

"In a way," he agreed. "Then she'd come to visit, and I'd be so angry that I would barely talk to her. It wasn't helpful. It didn't make me feel any better. I just didn't know any other way to deal with it." Noah cleared his throat. "I'm sorry, I'm not sure that's helpful for my brother—"

"It helps me know you better," she said quietly.

Did he dare show her more of what was inside him? He was supposed to be building his brother up, not exposing his own personal pain.

"Do you think your *mamm* will ever leave again?" she asked.

Noah let out a slow breath. "I hope not. I'm not sure I could take it."

That was all he had—a truly sincere hope that his *mamm* was back for good. She said she was, but was he confident of that? *Mamm* still wasn't like the other Amish women. She didn't have that quiet, unshakable confidence that other Amish women had, because she had been shaken.

Noah looked down at Eve's hand in his. The wind was cold, and he flipped the blanket over their entwined fingers.

"I'm afraid I'm making our family sound less devoted than it is," he said quietly. "You've seen the worst of us—I promise you that."

Eve didn't answer, but she did lean into his shoulder, the pressure of her arm against his feeling like an undeserved comfort. He wasn't supposed to be taking this from her…he was supposed to be the strong one. He was supposed to be doing this for Thomas.

"We love each other," he added earnestly. "And we care enough to stick around and work it out. I think that should count for something."

"It does."

He could sense the hesitation in her words, though.

"What do you think of us Wiebes now?"

Eve looked over at him, then sucked in a breath. "I thought I'd prepared myself to feel some jealousy."

"Yah?" He looked down at her.

"Do you know what it's like to look at the woman who might be the *mamm* who raises your baby? To look her in the face and know that your child will run to her with a skinned knee, and cry for her after a bad dream at night..."

"No," he breathed. "I guess I don't."

"My aunt warned me about how it might feel, and I thought I may be ready to face my own jealousy and pettiness." She dropped her gaze. "It turns out that it's scarier to see real people who might make mistakes, just like I would. Much scarier. I want my child to be insulated from anything that might hurt him. If I'm giving this baby up, that guarantee would make it easier. But instead I have to choose from very real, imperfect people."

"I'm sorry we aren't more perfect," he said quietly.

She smiled at that, but didn't answer. For a few minutes they rode in silence, their hands clasped under the blanket. He ran his thumb over her soft skin and looked over at her. He wished he could put his arm around her, tug her a little closer, but he was already overstepping by holding her hand, and while he should let go of her, he couldn't quite bring himself to do it.

They were quickly approaching the Glick house, and he let the horses slow just a little.

"You don't have to choose them," Noah said, looking over at her.

Eve's face was pale, and the headlamps reflected

off her face, making her eyes look bigger. She was beautiful—distractingly, heart-stoppingly beautiful.

"But you want me to," Eve whispered. "Even my aunt wants me to choose them."

Everyone wanted the ultimate sacrifice from Eve, and Noah had to wonder if there was anyone in her life right now who wasn't wanting to take this child from her...

"I want you to do what's right for you," he said earnestly. "And I mean that. *Yah*, my brother and his wife want to grow their family, but I want you to make the choice that feels right in your heart. I want you to find some peace—if you can."

"You won't try to convince me?" she asked.

"No. I know I've been talking my brother up, and he is a good man, but this isn't about how good or proper Thomas and Patience are. This isn't even about our family and what we can offer...or what we can't! It's about you—what you want."

Eve smiled faintly, and she looked like she was about to say something; her lips parted, but then she shut them and a strange little smile turned up the corners. He wasn't sure what had pleased her, but at least he'd been a part of it. Eve turned forward. He wished she'd look at him again, but the Glicks' drive was right ahead, and he pulled his hand back to take full control of the reins as he guided the horses into the turn.

"I know we keep saying that if you need anything, you should ask us," Noah said as they rolled toward the house. "But I'm here for you—me, personally. I mean, regardless of your choice. If you said right now that you'd chosen another family, I still want you to tell me if I can make any of this easier for you."

He reined in the horses just shy of the house lights. He wanted just one more minute with her. There was so much to say, and yet he didn't have the words to say it. There was something about Eve that tugged at him, that hinted at more just beneath the surface, and even though he knew that whatever friendship they formed would be cut off the minute she left Redemption, he couldn't bring himself to stop yet.

"What do you need?" he asked softly.

"I don't know..." Eve's eyes sparkled with unshed tears. "I think I need a friend."

"You have that," he said earnestly. "If I count at all..."

"We are very unlikely friends," she whispered.

He reached up and moved a tendril of stray hair off her forehead.

"I didn't expect to feel what I do when I'm with you—" He swallowed the words. He didn't know how to name what he felt.

His gaze dropped to her lips, and for a brief, insane moment, he imagined what it might feel like to kiss them. He touched her soft, chilled cheek with the back of one finger, and then let his hand drop—afraid to give in to any more temptation. What was it about this woman that drew him in this way? She was the mother of the child his brother hoped to adopt. Noah wasn't supposed to complicate her life!

"What do you feel?" she whispered.

"Like I want to be the one to take care of you," he said.

She dropped her gaze. What did she think of that—was it laughable?

"If I weren't expecting a baby, and if I'd met you at a hymn sing, I'd be soaring to hear you say that," she said, and he saw a smile tickle her lips.

"But everything is complicated, and we haven't just come back from a hymn sing," he said.

"No, we haven't." The smiled dropped, and she looked over at him sadly. "I should go in."

"*Yah.* Of course," he said, tearing his gaze from her face. "Let me help you down."

The front door to the house opened, and Lovina appeared in the glowing doorway. The kerosene lamps were lit throughout the bottom story, and candles flickered in the window, illuminating those evergreen sprigs tied with red ribbon.

Noah couldn't waste any more time, and he waited until Eve scooted over and he gave her a hand down. She stayed in his arms for only a moment, and then she stepped aside.

"Thank you for driving her, Noah!" Lovina called from the step.

Any privacy they might have had was spent, and Noah forced a smile and gave Lovina a wave.

"Anytime, Lovina!" he called back.

As if that was all that happened in his buggy tonight, and he hadn't told Eve what was happening inside him. When he looked toward Eve again, she gave him a private little smile.

"Good night, Eve," he said softly.

Eve didn't answer, and she headed toward the front

door, following the packed path through the snow. He watched until she got to the step, and then turned away.

Eve had much to discuss with her aunt tonight, and it would be none of his business—none of his family's business. Her choice was going to be an intensely personal one, and all he could do was pray the prayer Patience had suggested—that *Gott* would do right by all of them...especially Eve.

Chapter Seven

Aunt Lovina held the door as Eve went inside the house. The smell of percolating coffee filled the interior, and the sound of chatting voices filtered through the sitting room from the kitchen. Eve paused to slip out of her uncle's coat and hang it on a hook, and then step out of her boots, leaving them on a mat to absorb the melting snow.

She looked behind her at the buggy now disappearing up the drive, the headlamps bopping along with the rhythm of the horses. Noah had said he felt something for her…and the timing was terrible—impossible, really. But he'd said it, and she tucked his words away inside her heart.

"How did it go?" Lovina asked quietly.

"I learned about Rachel Wiebe," Eve said.

"Oh…" Lovina's face pinked and she nodded. "*Yah*. Rachel."

"You didn't tell me?" Eve met her aunt's gaze. "You said this was a good family, and you didn't share a detail like that?"

"It's complicated, dear," Lovina replied. "Rachel's back. We have to forgive, don't we? If we hold on to anger and resentment—"

"This is the family you recommended," Eve said.

"I know…and I still do. They're good people, Eve. I promise you." Lovina looked over her shoulder hurriedly. "But we don't have time to talk about that this minute—we have company."

Ruby came into the sitting room just then, Rebecca in tow. They were both carrying platters of Christmas cookies, and they smiled when they saw Eve.

"You're in time for cookies," Ruby said. "And mint tea if you don't want to stay awake until the crack of dawn with coffee. Wollie's here!"

"Wollie?" Eve suddenly felt very tired.

"Come, let's get you something to eat," Lovina said quietly. "I have a feeling you haven't eaten much…"

"No, I didn't," Eve admitted. "Thank you."

Wollie, as it turned out, had come in this direction to see a little house that was for rent. He had to find a home now, and this one was available.

After everyone chatted and played some card games, Eve found herself alone with her cousin in the sitting room.

"So will you come back?" Eve asked him.

"I don't know…"

"We heard that you wanted to," she said. "Everyone here has been praying for it."

She'd been praying for it, too.

"It's not so simple," he said. "My wife isn't Amish, and my *kinner* are old enough to remember not being Amish…"

"You think they won't be accepted?" she asked.

"I think they might be angry at me," he said, his voice low. "I think Caleb, my oldest son, might have a few opinions of his own right now."

"He's not even ten," Eve said.

"Don't underestimate a boy's ability to hold a grudge." But Wollie smiled while he said it. "You don't need to worry about me, Eve. You've got enough on your plate."

"Why did you go?" she asked. "You left right after visiting us, and for a few years after that I blamed myself. I thought I'd talked too much about rebellious ways."

"Evie," Wollie said softly, shaking his head. "This isn't something I like to spread around, but Natasha was already pregnant with Caleb at that point. I'd been working with your *daet* because he was paying me, and I needed the money to marry Natasha and support her. It wasn't you. My decision was already made."

Eve shrugged. "I didn't know she was pregnant…but I had figured out it wasn't a thirteen-year-old's flawed logic that chased you off."

Wollie chuckled. "That's good. And for the record, I'm fine, Eve. I promise. And I love my wife and my children. I'm more worried about you right now. You've come here to have the baby and…give it up."

She nodded. "That's the plan."

Wollie was silent for a moment. "Have you considered…other options?"

"Like going English?" she asked bitterly. "It was an Englisher boy who did this—against my will. I'm not going there."

"They aren't all the same," Wollie said. "And a single mother might be able to raise her child."

She met his gaze, but didn't answer, and his cheeks pinked.

"Right…" he said. "That's too far."

"Why did you go English? Just for…her?" Eve asked hesitantly.

"*Yah*, and because I didn't see a life for myself at home," Wollie said. "I wanted options. I felt constrained, like there was only one path for me and I had no choices left."

"But you did say you wanted to come back…"

Wollie blew out a slow breath, then leaned his elbows onto his knees. "I miss it. I miss our way of life, our pace of life… I miss knowing what's right and what's wrong. But now, I'm thinking things through, I guess. I came here to see my aunt, and there is that little farmhouse that came available to rent. They go fast in these parts—if I want it, I have to move quickly. It would be a nice change for us, I think—getting back to the earth again."

"What does Natasha think of that?" Eve asked.

He shook his head. "I don't know. I'm afraid to ask. I love her with all my heart, Eve, but we're very different. I want some space to breathe, some chickens, maybe a cow or two. She wants convenience. And I don't blame her—but even the thought of raising chickens intimidates her. Right now, we might not have a lot of choice, though. We need a home, and this is available. And I can't be cooped up in an apartment with four *kinner*. I'll go crazy."

Wollie and Natasha would be very different—

an Englisher woman and an Amish man. Wollie hadn't fully transformed into an Englisher, either. He still had the slow movements, the thoughtful way about him that distinguished him from regular Englishers. It wasn't just about the clothes or the electricity.

"You think it's too late?" she asked.

"I think it might be," he said with a nod. "Right now, I need a home for my family. I'm married now—I made my choice."

Eve's heart might be breaking, but she had a chance at an Amish marriage still. Wollie had taken those vows, and he couldn't try again in the Amish community if it didn't work with Natasha. Marriage was for life for the Amish, wherever that marriage took place. He'd chosen an Englisher life, and even if he longed to return to his Amish roots, it wasn't only about him anymore. He now had a family.

"I can pray for you anyway," Eve said.

"Thank you," Wollie said, casting her a sad smile. "I'll pray for you, too."

For whatever it was worth—because they were both in impossible situations. Maybe *Gott*'s best had changed for Wollie, too. No matter how much wisdom they'd gained along the way, there was no undoing the choices that had led them here.

There was the sound of a buggy coming into the drive, and they both looked out the living room window to see Uncle Hezekiah returning from his shift at the canning plant. It was time for the family to come together and enjoy the time they had. This was what Christmas was all about, wasn't it? Gathering with family and leaving the impossible in *Gott*'s hands.

The next day, Eve went with her aunt and her cousin Ruby into the shop. Rebecca was staying home to take care of the housework, and Ruby brought her cross-stitching with her, attempting to finish the job that morning between helping customers. Rebecca had finished hers the day before, and Lovina already had it on display when she flicked the sign to Open.

"Wollie's very nice," Ruby said, settling down with her needle.

"He always was," Eve replied. "He was always easy to talk to. He's decent."

"What's his Englisher wife like?" Ruby asked.

Eve shook her head. "She's…English."

How to describe a woman that different? She was everything they were not, from the blue jeans down to the way she talked. She was uncomfortably open.

Lovina came past with a bolt of fabric under one arm. She gave her daughter a meaningful look.

"I think it's good that you saw Wollie for yourself, my dear girl. You just remember how hard it is to even visit your family once you've gone English. It's painful, and Wollie has to live with the consequences."

"Won't his parents even see him?" Ruby asked.

"Oh, they will, but they won't be happy with his choices, either," Lovina said. "He visits them from time to time, but there is no warm affection between his mother and his wife. How can there be? They're as different as night and day."

"Maybe in time—" Ruby started.

"Ruby." Lovina fixed her with a serious look. "Can you imagine what it would be like not to see me anymore? Can you imagine not seeing your *daet*, or having babies and having them never really know us? It would break my heart, for sure. And I think it would break yours, too. There are some mistakes that you just can't undo."

Ruby's glance flickered in Eve's direction, and Eve felt her cheeks heat. Like her own situation—that was true, this baby was coming and there was no undoing that.

"I can help with the cross-stitching," Eve offered, eager to change the subject.

"Would you?" Ruby passed it over. "My fingers are in agony. I can hardly hold a needle anymore."

Eve looked at the pattern so far, and then the nearly finished project that was neatly stretched out on a hoop. There wasn't much left to finish—just one piece of holly—and Eve settled in, counting stitches on the pattern, and then on the cloth, before she began to work.

Eve didn't really enjoy cross-stitching, but keeping her fingers busy seemed to be a good distraction, and she worked on the last of the cross-stitching while her aunt and cousin waited on customers.

The day was a busy one—Christmas being right around the corner—and most of the clientele were English looking for gifts for their friends and families. Eve watched the people as they flowed through the shop, stitching until the piece was complete, and when she snipped the last thread, running her fingers over her handiwork, the bell tinkled above the door. She looked up to see Patience Wiebe come into the shop.

Eve's breath caught. Patience…she'd want an answer, wouldn't she?

"Hello," Patience said cheerily. "How are you, Lovina?

Hi, Ruby!" Then her gaze swept over to where Eve sat, and Patience's expression shifted to something less confident. "Hello, Eve."

Another customer came up to the counter and Lovina had to serve her. Eve put down the needlework and rose to her feet.

"Hello," she said. "I should thank you for dinner last night. It was delicious."

Did she sound sincere? Eve had all but run for the door the night before, and while it was her opinion of the Wiebe family that mattered in the adoption, she did have enough good character to care what they thought of her.

"I'm here to see you, actually," Patience said, coming toward her. "I don't feel like that dinner went very well, and—" Patience lowered her voice when she noticed Ruby watching them curiously "—I was hoping we could talk, just the two of us."

Eve hesitated. "I don't have an answer for you, if that's what you've come for."

"That's actually a relief, because if you'd made your decision after last night, I feel like it wouldn't have gone in our favor," Patience said. "I just wanted to explain our family, maybe. Or…show you who I am without a meal and a family around me. Just me."

Eve nodded. "All right."

"I was going to pick some lunch up for my husband, Noah and Amos," Patience said. "Would you like to come with me?"

"*Yah*, I suppose," Eve agreed. "Let me get my coat."

Another few customers came into the shop, distracting Ruby, and allowing Eve and Patience to leave without further notice. When they got out into the street, their breath stood in the air in front of them.

"It seems that no one told you about my mother-in-law," Patience said as they headed down the sidewalk. "I thought your aunt might."

"She didn't," Eve replied. "But Noah filled me in a little bit more on the ride home."

"She's a very loving woman," Patience said. "And our family had to deal with a lot of hurt feelings and old grudges when Rachel returned. I think we've done well, though. And we have to forgive."

"Yah," Eve said. "And I have to think of my child."

"You do." Patience gave her a sad look. "I understand that. I suppose I was hoping that it might help you in your decision if you got to know me a little bit. Most of that dinner seemed focused on my mother-in-law."

Eve smiled at that. "It was, wasn't it?"

They looked both ways before crossing the street, and when they reached the opposite sidewalk, Eve tugged her shawl a little closer.

"Would you like to know about me?" Patience asked hopefully.

"Yah," Eve replied. "I would."

"My family had eight *kinner* in it," Patience said. "I got sick in my teens, and I had to have a surgery that… it left me unable to have *kinner* of my own." Patience's gaze flickered in Eve's direction, and color rose in her cheeks. "It broke my heart. I loved children so much, and I wanted my own babies. But *Gott* sometimes takes things away, doesn't He? So I decided to teach school. It was partly because it would let me be with *kinner* again, and partly because I had to turn down a man who proposed very sincerely."

"Why did you turn him down?" Eve asked, slowing her steps.

"Because he wanted more children, and I couldn't give him that," Patience replied. "He was very excited at the thought of more children, and while he might have married me anyway, I didn't want to be the wife who let him down."

"I can understand that," Eve replied softly.

"So when I met Thomas, I was convinced it would be the same—he had Rue and he longed to have more *kinner*. Rue needed siblings to help her settle in as an Amish child, and…and once again I couldn't give that."

"Why did you marry Thomas, then?" Eve asked.

"Because I met an older couple who had never had *kinner* of their own, but who had lived such a full and loving life by opening their home to young people who needed love and support, and I realized that there were other ways to live a happy life." Patience stopped and turned toward Eve. She crossed her arms over her chest and shivered. "I think *Gott* works in mysterious ways, and He puts people together for a reason."

"'God setteth the solitary in families,'" Eve quoted the verse from scripture.

"I'm not a perfect *mamm* or wife, and maybe you saw that," Patience said, her voice shaking. "Maybe you don't think I'd be good enough for your little one—"

"No one is perfect," Eve replied. "And that is probably the scariest part. I have to choose a real, honest woman to be my baby's *mamm*. And she'll make mistakes."

"I'd certainly do my best not to," Patience said quietly. "But you're right. I'm only human."

"I hadn't counted on this being so hard," Eve admitted softly.

"Are you giving this baby up?" Patience asked.

"I have to."

"Is there anything I can do to make it easier for you?" Patience asked. "I'd send you letters, if you wanted. I'd send you locks of hair, little handprints—"

"No." Eve cleared her throat. "No. If I do this, it has to be complete. I can't drag my heart after your family. I'd have to let go."

An icy wind wound around them, and they started walking again up the street. Eve couldn't have any emotional connections to the Wiebes if she left this child with them—and that included Noah. Whatever had started to stew between them needed to stop. She was in Redemption for one heartbreaking reason—and she couldn't allow herself to form attachments.

They went into a restaurant, and Patience ordered food to go. She ordered a meal for Eve, too, and when they had collected the foam containers and were ready to head back, the wind had let up somewhat, and some watery sunlight sparkled through the clouds, warming the air just enough to take the sting out of the cold. They headed back down the sidewalk, each of them carrying two bags of food. A wagon with jingling bells on the horse's harness came past them, the wagon filled with laughing Englishers. The side of the wagon read Eli's Christmas Wagon Rides, and Eve forced a smile in return to a small Englisher boy who beamed at her, waving as they passed.

"You have a lot of connections with the English," Eve said. "I have to admit, that makes me nervous. Especially with this child being half-English, I'm afraid that there will be a pull of some sort, tugging my child back to them."

"I knew a boy once who was adopted from the English and grew up Amish," Patience said. "I went to school with him. He wanted to know about the family that gave him up, and his Amish parents wouldn't tell him anything. They simply said that he was adopted, and they loved him, and what was in the past was in the past."

"That sounds proper," Eve said.

"It wasn't what he needed, though," Patience replied. "He needed to know the truth, to have information. He ended up leaving during his *Rumspringa*, and he went off to find his Englisher mother."

"Did he find her?" Eve asked.

"No, he didn't. And he didn't come back, either. He came to visit once every long while, but he never came back for good."

Like Wollie? He had been born Amish, but his visits were infrequent, and they seemed to be laced with sadness.

Eve sighed. "Why does that Englisher life tug at people that way?"

"I think it only tugs at people if it stays a mystery," Patience said. "For what it's worth, I have a daughter who is half-English, my husband's daughter from a previous relationship, but she feels like mine. And I'm afraid sometimes of the exact same thing—that the Englishers will tug at some private place in her heart.

And I know that telling you this won't help my cause, but it's true. I worry. But I've also given it a lot of thought, and people are drawn to mysteries. But mysteries are only intriguing until they come out into the light. When you learn the full truth about something and are allowed to look at it straight, you realize that it isn't quite so alluring, after all."

"And so with Rue—"

"She remembers her Englisher *mamm*. She knows her *mamm* loved her dearly and that Thomas is her father. She knows I'm her stepmother, and that I love her, too. We talk about Tina—Rue's *mamm*—and we don't make mention of her as something bad or uncomfortable. Tina will always be part of Rue's heart. Always."

"Do you think it will keep her Amish?" Eve asked.

"I hope so. I love her like my own, and I'll continue to love her with everything I have. If love is enough to keep a child in our way of life, she'll have more love in her life than she will know what to do with."

"And if you adopted this baby..." Eve asked softly.

"We would do the same," Patience replied. "We'd tell this child that his *mamm* couldn't take care of him. That it wasn't her fault and she loved him so much that she allowed him to grow up with us. And I'd love him with all my heart."

"And if he came looking for me one day?" Eve asked, and she felt a swell of hope that she couldn't tamp down, no matter how hard she tried.

"Then I would welcome the chance to have you back in my kitchen," Patience said, stopping to meet Eve's gaze. "And you and I would be family in a different kind of way. But you would never be hidden away as a dark secret. You'd be in our hearts—in your child's heart—and I would never compete for that love. Your child would be loved from all sides."

"If I—" Eve swallowed. "If I made a little quilt—"

"I'd let him know that you'd made it for him," Patience whispered. "And I'd let him know that his birth *mamm* prayed for him with every beat of her heart that he'd grow up to be good and kind and honest."

Lovina had thought that sending a little gift would be a mistake, but talking with Patience, it didn't seem like such a mistake. And maybe Patience was right about the mystery.

"Just one thing," Eve said, lowering her voice. "I never want my child to know about the father. To know his father was such a despicable man—"

"I agree there," Patience said with a nod. "That would be a conversation that you could have with him later, but I wouldn't tell that story."

"Or her…" Eve said faintly.

"Or her." Patience smiled hopefully. "If this child needed more answers to stay decidedly Amish, then I would write to you. We'd do the best we could for this child together, you and me. I'd love this baby well, Eve."

Eve slid her hand over her belly, feeling the shifting of this infant inside her. Of the families she could choose from, even with their very human foibles, the Wiebe family was the best choice. Her child wouldn't be just accepted, her baby would be longed for and deeply loved. And Patience had a heart big enough to embrace the birth mothers of her *kinner*, too. That was more than Eve had expected to find for her child's future home.

"I know I have to make a choice…" Eve said slowly.

"And I've put it off because it made it easier somehow to avoid what I have to do, but I know I can't keep doing that. This baby will arrive soon, and when it does, it needs a mother."

Tears welled in Eve's eyes at the thought. She would give birth, and she'd have to say her goodbyes.

"I'm not pressuring you," Patience said softly.

"I choose you," Eve said, swallowing the lump in her throat.

Patience put her bags down on the sidewalk, tears welling in her eyes.

"*Yah?* Me and Thomas?"

Eve nodded, and Patience stepped forward and wrapped her arms around Eve's neck in a fierce hug.

"Thank you," Patience breathed. "Thank you so much, Eve. We'll do well by you, and by your baby— I promise!"

The plane bit into the wood, shaving off a golden curl. With every heave, another one slipped to the floor, gathering in a tumbled heap at Noah's feet. He had always liked the smell of freshly shaved wood, and when he paused to test the surface, he heard the sound of voices from inside the showroom. More customers, no doubt. Thomas was already out there.

Noah hadn't been great company today. He'd been thinking about that buggy ride home—the one where he'd said too much and held Eve's hand as if they were courting. He wasn't being appropriate—on any level! This woman wasn't available, especially not to the brother of the man who hoped to adopt her baby. He'd been out of line, and he felt like a fool for having let himself go there, especially at such a sensitive time.

Noah leaned into the labor again, and as he did so, his gaze moved over to the little cradle Thomas had been working on between customers' orders. It wasn't anywhere near done—still rough, and the pieces had been put together to test the fit, but the next step was to take it all apart again to smooth everything down and sand it.

Thomas hadn't said anything about that little crib, and it wasn't an order—that was for certain—so he didn't have to explain himself. This was a baby's bed, just in case they needed one in the next couple of weeks.

Noah felt a wave of guilt. Thomas and Patience had already fallen in love with this baby—or the idea of the baby, perhaps. Their hopes were soaring up along with their prayers. Was Noah messing this up? He hadn't been talking to Eve on their behalf last night. He'd been opening up because it felt good to talk to her, and somehow opening up to Eve was feeling all too natural. That wasn't helping his brother's cause.

The door to the workshop opened and Thomas stuck his head inside, a beaming smile on his face.

"Noah, come out here!" Thomas said.

Noah put down the plane and grabbed a towel to wipe the wood dust from his hands and arms.

"What's going on?" Noah asked.

"Just come out here!" Thomas disappeared again, and Noah headed for the door. Maybe there was someone he hadn't seen in a long time, or a gift from a neighbor? Noah attempted to put himself into a better mood to be sociable, and when he pushed open the door that led to the showroom, he saw Patience and Eve standing there with bags of food from a local restaurant.

"This is nice," Noah said. "Tell me you aren't just teasing us with all that food."

Eve looked up when he said that, and she lifted a bag in his direction. Her expression was solemn, and he moved over to where she stood.

"Is it okay if we tell our family?" Patience asked.

Noah took the bag that Eve held out to him, his fingers lingering over hers. She pulled her hand back, then smiled faintly. "That would be fine."

"Eve has chosen us to be the family for her baby," Thomas said with a grin, but his smile slipped when he looked back to Eve. "Eve, I can't tell you what this means to us. And we can promise you that we'll love this child with everything we have, and we'll raise him or her to be godly and honest and good. Thank you. From the bottom of our hearts. Thank you."

She had made her decision? Noah's gaze whipped to Eve, who stood as still as a post, her hand now on top of the dome of her belly.

"Love this child well," she said, her voice tight. "That's all I can ask."

For the next few minutes there was some excited talking. Patience and Thomas looked at each other with such happiness in their eyes that Noah had to look away from the intimacy of the moment. This was a happy day for Thomas and Patience, but he could see the way Eve stood—still as stone, but for the flutter of her pulse at the base of her pale neck. She'd made her choice, but that didn't mean it had been easy for her.

Noah touched her elbow and Eve looked toward him.

"I suppose you'll be happy," Eve said quietly.

"Are *you*?" he asked, frowning.

"No," she said. "But it's the right thing to do."

Of course, it wouldn't be a happy day for her, and Noah felt the imbalance in the room—Thomas and Patience's elation compared to Eve's crushing sadness. Could he really expect anything different?

"We should probably keep this quiet for now," Patience said. "Let's keep it to our family only—Amos and *Mammi* included, of course—but other than that, we can tell people after the baby has arrived."

Eve didn't answer, but she nodded, and her face went just a little bit paler. He put his hand out and touched her elbow again. He could claim that he was afraid she was going to faint, but truthfully, he just wanted to touch her—reassure her that she wasn't alone in this, maybe. Let her know that one person in this room understood how much this hurt her.

What was it like for her to have everyone celebrating the baby she'd have to give up? Noah couldn't even imagine what she must be feeling right now, but when Thomas and Patience turned toward each other again, Noah tugged Eve aside.

"Are you all right?" he asked quietly, searching her face for some deeper feelings—some strength, perhaps, that she was holding in reserve.

"I will be," she said, and tears sparkled in her eyes. "It's good to know this child is wanted by so many people."

She met his gaze, and he could see the clashing emotions swimming there. She looked away and seemed to steel herself.

"I'm going to be seeing your cousin on Monday—I'm dropping off some things when they move into that farmhouse," Noah said.

She looked up at him mutely. He didn't know why he was doing this—it was all he had to offer. He wanted to spend some time with her, and maybe give her some distraction from this painful time. And he had so little that he could offer her...

"Will you come with me?" Noah asked.

"*Yah*, I will," Eve said, and she swallowed hard.

"Are you coming to Service Sunday tomorrow?" Noah asked.

She nodded. "*Yah*, I'll be there."

"Maybe I can get you to take a walk with me. Get away from everyone for a while."

"That would be worth more than you know." Eve seemed to rally herself, standing a little taller.

"Are you sure you're okay?" he asked uncertainly.

"I will be. I just need to be alone for a little bit." She pressed her lips together. "I'm going back to my aunt's shop now."

"Sure."

Eve slipped along the edge of the shop, past the display headboards and footboards, and had almost made it to the outside door when Thomas looked up. Eve didn't stop—didn't explain herself. She just pushed outside, the cold wind billowing her dress behind her as she walked outside, and passed in front of the window before disappearing from sight.

"Was it something we said?" Thomas asked, his expression turned worried.

"I think she just needs to be alone," Noah replied. "As joyful as it is for you two, it's a sacrifice for her."

Noah met his brother's gaze, and Thomas looked back toward the window again. He and Patience leaned toward each other, their arms brushing as they looked in the direction Eve had gone.

"I don't think it's possible to make this any easier for her," Patience said. "But should I go after her, or—"

Thomas looked helplessly toward Noah.

"I don't think so," Noah said. *Let her cry in peace.*

"Let me show you something I've been working on," Thomas said softly to his wife.

As Thomas and Patience went into the workshop, Noah stood in the empty showroom, watching out the window as some people, laden with shopping bags, dashed across the slushy street. This Christmas would be a new beginning for his brother, but it would be a tragic goodbye for Eve.

Her sacrifice was making a dream of a family come true for Thomas and Patience, and while they excitedly got ready for this baby, Eve needed someone to care for her, too.

Until she left them all behind to restart her life, was it terribly stupid if he wanted to be that man?

Chapter Eight

Service Sunday was always a day that Eve had looked forward to in years past. It was a chance to see friends and extended family, to catch up on gossip, and worship. But today, as the buggy rattled down the road and she watched the scenery pass from her seat squeezed in next to her aunt and uncle, the horses clopping comfortably through the winter morning, Eve's mind was on the family she'd left behind seven months earlier when *Daet* sent her to stay with a distant cousin of his. But when *Daet* asked Aunt Lovina for confidential advice, Lovina had insisted that Eve come stay the rest of the time with her. Eve was glad for that now—she felt more emotional support with Lovina than she had in the other community.

How was *Daet* doing on his own? She'd gotten a few letters from him, but he was never one to complain. He just said that all was well and told her of the things he was looking forward to once she was home again. Her siblings seemed to be doing fine—one of her brothers bought a new buggy. Life was plodding along back in her hometown, and when she returned, there would be a place for her again, but she wouldn't be able to breathe a word about the baby she'd left behind.

Maybe she could talk to *Daet*, but she didn't want to put more pressure onto his shoulders. He wanted things to go back to normal. He wanted her to see her friends, to get to know some nice young men and to carry on as if this visit was simply an extended stay with some family.

Could she do it? Would seeing her friends again make all of this seem like a bad dream? She could only hope.

The baby moved. There wasn't as much space anymore for kicks, but she could feel the extension of a foot pushing up into her ribs, and she smoothed a hand over her belly. Everything would be fine—wouldn't it? This baby would be loved, she would get her second chance at a proper Amish life and a family's prayers for another child were about to be answered through her.

It just didn't feel fine. It *hurt*.

Gott, please make this easier... I'm trying to do the right thing.

Lately, she'd been thinking about Hannah from the Bible—Samuel's mother. She'd longed for a baby of her own, and she'd prayed for one, but she'd also made a promise to *Gott* that if He gave her a child, she'd give him back to the Lord. How could a mother make a promise like that? But she had—and she'd stood by her word and sent him away to live with the priest when he was just a little boy.

Hannah's heart would have been in shreds—but *Gott* rewarded her with more *kinner*.

Would Eve be like Hannah—a woman whose heart was broken by keeping a promise? If she was, maybe *Gott* would reward her like Hannah, too, and give her the honest home complete with husband and children that she so desperately longed for.

And the price would be this child that had been forced upon her…this child she couldn't help but love with all her heart.

The buggy turned into a drive, and her eyes moved over the familiar scene of an Amish farm set up for Sunday services. A field was already filled with buggies from neighboring Amish homes, and the horses were in the field beyond, a pile of dried silage and a watering trough already set out for them.

In the back of the buggy, Ruby and Rebecca chattered on about someone's handsome cousin who was visiting from another community. From what Eve could gather, the boy was far too old for either of them, and while the girls admitted this, they still wanted a chance to see him themselves.

"Emma said he has red hair." Ruby sighed. "And green eyes."

"I don't know any Amish boys with red hair!" her sister said. "I think that's an exaggeration. But I do know that he's tall and handsome. Naomi Zook said he was at her farm helping with some broken fences, and she talked to him for five whole minutes while he had some pie before he left, and—"

"Enough of that," Lovina said sharply, looking over her shoulder. "You aren't old enough for courting, so I suggest you leave it to those who are!"

"It's just that we heard there aren't enough girls

his age he isn't related to in his community—" Ruby started.

"And you aren't his age, either!" Lovina retorted. "I don't think you're going to be much help to him, are you?"

Eve smiled at the exchange. Her own *mamm* had given her own little lectures when Eve was as young as her cousins were now. Girls were never quite so grown up as they believed themselves to be.

When Uncle Hezekiah parked the buggy and let the horses into the pasture beyond, her aunt helped her get down from the buggy, and then both let out a sigh once her feet were solidly on the ground. Ruby and Rebecca headed off to find their friends, leaving Eve with her aunt.

"I can introduce you to some people," Lovina said.

"I'd rather not, actually," Eve said. "I'll come sit with you when the service starts, though."

"How are you feeling?" her aunt asked. "Any twinges lately? Any discomfort?"

Lovina had given birth enough times of her own to know the early signs. Eve shook her head. "Nothing. I feel…cumbersome, but that's about it."

Lovina smiled wanly. "I know that feeling, too." She looked over toward another arriving family. "Dear, I need to talk to Emma—I'm going to be helping her host a quilting day."

"Go ahead, I'll be fine," Eve said with a smile. "I'm going to go find a washroom at the house."

Her aunt smiled. "I'll see you later, then. We've got a fair amount of time before the service starts."

Eve breathed out a sigh as she escaped from her

aunt's well-meant friendliness and headed toward the house. Eve hadn't told her family that she'd made her choice. It wasn't that she thought she'd change her mind, but she hadn't had the heart to discuss it all over again, so she'd simply not mentioned it.

She'd tell her aunt tonight—she'd have to soon. This baby was due any day now, and Christmas was this upcoming week.

Eve didn't actually need to use the washroom—it was just an excuse, a mission to head out on that would let her spend some time on her own before she was squeezed onto a bench with her aunt, cousins and a multitude of women she didn't know.

A few young men came ambling past her—one of whom was rather tall, and if she wasn't mistaken, appeared to have red hair. Maybe Emma Zook was more truthful than they'd thought. The young men didn't take any notice of her, but there was a woman with three preteen girls who looked her over with prim disapproval.

Eve gave a nod and smiled, hoping to disarm her with a bit of pleasantness, but as they passed her, Eve could overhear the woman speaking, even with her voice lowered.

"...and that is why you don't toy with boys too early, girls." More girls mooning over the redheaded boy from another community? Eve couldn't help but smile at that. But the woman's next words drained her humor. "You see that pregnant girl? That's shameful, is what that is. She's here to have her baby because she has no husband. And she'll have to give it up. That's what comes of doing things the wrong way..."

Eve couldn't make out the rest of the woman's words,

but tears misted her eyes and she struggled to maintain some decorum. This was precisely why she needed a fresh start of her own—people would never forget, and whether or not it was fair, she'd be used as their walking lessons for their *kinner*, the warning against what could happen to misbehaving young people.

Shameful. She didn't even feel angry at that word, although she'd have every right to it. This wasn't her fault, but even if she'd been the one to make a mistake, was this not punishment enough? That woman would never know the ache of loss that Eve was going to experience. Couldn't that morality lesson have waited until she was at least out of earshot?

"Eve?"

Eve blinked through the tears in her eyes and looked up in surprise to find Noah coming out of the house, dressed in somber black. He was different than she'd gotten used to seeing him around his workplace. He looked so much more proper in his Sunday black with the woolen coat. His gaze moved over her face, and then he looked around them, his attention landing in the direction of the retreating woman with her daughters.

"What happened?" he asked.

"It's—" Eve swallowed. "It's nothing."

"It doesn't look like nothing," he replied. "You're crying."

"I'm being used as a morality lesson for some girls," Eve said hollowly.

Noah's expression clouded and his jaw tensed. "That's wrong."

"I agree, but I can't do a whole lot about it, can I?"

What was he going to do, chase a woman down and tell her off? Not likely.

"I promised you a walk," he said.

"Now?" she asked. "Isn't service about to start?"

"It's up to you," he replied. "Whatever will make you feel better right now."

She didn't actually want to go sit on a bench and pretend she didn't feel the eyes boring into her. She didn't want to try not to be selectively deaf to the whispers. She'd wanted to come to Service Sunday so she could worship, but she might have been better off staying home. Noah's offer of a walk was a rather tempting one. A few snowflakes danced through the air, spinning and pirouetting their way to the snowy ground.

"All right," Eve said. "I think I'd like that. But I can't walk very far."

"You tell me how far you want to walk," he said. "And I'll carry you back, if I have to."

She smiled in spite of herself at that mental image. He was joking, obviously, but the thought of being in his arms was a rather cozy one.

"It'll be in sight of anyone who cares to check up on us," he added.

She smiled wistfully. "I don't think I'm any worry to the unmarried girls right now, Noah. I'm no one's competition."

But the way a smile quirked up one side of his mouth made her stomach flutter.

"You're the only one I'm out walking with," he said.

"Don't tease," she said.

Now was not the time to pretend that they were anything they were not. Her stay here was difficult enough as it was, and she wasn't in the mood for pointless flirting or untruths.

"I'm not teasing," he said, sobering. "I'm serious. I'm not taking anyone home from singing. I'm...very single."

So was she, for that matter, but she was leaving here sooner than later. And when she left, she'd leave her heart behind in a bundle of baby blankets, but she wouldn't be coming back.

"They'll still talk," she said quietly.

"Let them." His dark gaze locked on to hers and he raised an eyebrow. "Not everything that is said is worthy of being heard."

She felt a smile tug at her lips. Was this really the proper Noah Wiebe, unconcerned about gossip?

"All right. Then a walk would be very nice, Noah. Thank you."

A few spinning snowflakes danced in the air, but there was no wind, and as Noah and Eve walked up the drive together, Noah felt warm in his woolen coat. The last of the buggies had already arrived, and he and Eve ambled past some boys who were throwing snowballs at each other. He put up his gloved hand to bat one out of the air that was coming in Eve's direction.

"Sorry!" the boy called after them.

"Aim better!" Noah called back, and the boy who'd thrown the snowball got another one right in the chest. He couldn't help but chuckle. When he glanced down at Eve, she looked somber, though.

"I know that woman from earlier," Noah said. "The one with the three girls."

"I'm sure," Eve said dully.

"No, I mean—" Noah stepped closer to her, his arm brushing hers. "She's warning her daughters because she's had some difficult times of her own. Her twin sister got pregnant before marriage, and no one could figure out who the father was. We never did discover who had done it, and she went English."

"Oh." Eve looked up at him, her brow creasing. "So it was an Amish man who—"

"It seems," he replied. "But he wouldn't step up, and she wouldn't say who he was. She was only about sixteen at the time, and she had her baby, stayed home with her parents, and when the baby was a toddler, she took her child and left."

"What became of her?" Eve asked.

Noah shook his head. "I don't know. She'd be in her forties now. No one told me more than that. But I remember the huge scandal at the time."

"So she's afraid of her own girls making the mistake her sister did," Eve concluded.

"*Yah*. I don't think it's as personal as it feels…if that helps."

Because if he could help to deflect at least some of that insult, he'd feel better, too.

Eve sighed. "It does, actually."

"Do you ever get tempted to leave the Amish life?" he asked.

Eve looked over, surprised. "Why?"

"You could keep your child…" he said simply, and he eyed her, wondering if he'd just planted a seed of rebellion.

"No." She shook her head. "I wouldn't be here if I were willing to do it."

"Has it crossed your mind?" he asked.

"Honestly?" She glanced up at him. "*Yah.* It has. But I want an Amish life, and I love this baby too much to allow him or her to grow up out there with the Englishers. This isn't only for me, it's for my baby, too. I want an Amish life for both of us."

They reached the top of the drive, and a red pickup truck rumbled past with a husky in the back, its tongue lolling out happily. The snow started to fall a little thicker now, dampening the sound around them. They started up the road together, their boots leaving tracks in the newly fallen snow.

"I considered it—" Noah said, his voice low.

"Jumping the fence?" Eve asked, and he heard the surprise in her voice.

"Joining my *mamm*," he said. "A few times, in fact. I missed her so much, and once I even went so far as to pack a bag. I never told anyone that before. Not even her."

He looked down at Eve, and she shrugged weakly. "You're human, Noah. I'm glad you didn't go."

"Me, too..."

Another car came up the road, and as they stepped closer to the side, Eve's foot slipped, and he instinctively put his arm through hers to keep her up. For a moment, they stood like that, arms linked and his feet firmly planted to support them both. She looked up at him, her eyes wide in surprise.

"Careful," he murmured.

She laughed softly. "I almost fell."

"Not with me here," he said.

She straightened and pulled out of his arms. "You shouldn't flirt, Noah."

"I'm not," he replied. "I'm serious. As long as I'm here, I'm looking after you. And not for my brother, or for the sake of community, or anything else. I'm here for you."

Eve looked down, but she slid her hand into the crook of his arm, and the gentle pressure of her fingers against his coat felt good.

"We have a little bit of time together," he said. "And I know it isn't much, but I'm glad I've gotten to know you."

"Even if we can never speak again?" she asked. Her ears were getting red from the cold, but she didn't look up.

"Even then," he said quietly. "You deserve someone who cares, even for a little while."

Ahead, there was a vegetable stall, the little shack painted white and blending into the falling snow if it weren't for the hand-painted words in red on the side of it: Amish Home Grown Produce. In the summer, Englisher vehicles would park along the side of the road to come buy Amish fruits and vegetables. In the winter, that little shack stayed empty.

A brisk wind picked up, and Eve hunched her shoulders against it, moving closer to his arm. The snow, once falling lazily, whipped in a momentarily blinding haze around them, and Noah slowed.

"We should go back," Noah said, but when he looked the way they'd come, snow was blasting across the road in swirls of white. The wind had picked up faster than he'd anticipated, and it was probably stupid of him to bring a pregnant woman on a walk at this time of year. He'd been thinking of getting her away from the pressure, not dragging her through a blizzard.

"Let's just stop inside the veggie stand until this calms down a bit," she suggested.

"*Yah*, that's smart," he agreed, and they picked up their pace.

He fumbled with the latch, but once he flicked it open, Eve went into the little hut ahead of him, and he followed her, pulling the door shut behind them. Daylight streamed in through cracks in the wall, and a sifting of snow covered the bench along the back wall. Noah brushed it off, and Eve sat down with a sigh.

"I'm sorry to drag you out like this," he said.

"I wasn't dragged." Eve shot him a smile and put her hand over her coat-covered belly. "Everything is harder right now. I can barely take a full breath."

Noah sank onto the bench next to her. "Are you comfortable enough?"

"*Yah*, I'm fine. This is just part of being pregnant."

They were silent for a couple of beats, and Noah heard the rumble of a vehicle passing again. Her time here was short. She'd deliver soon, and then she'd go home, and he found himself feeling an aching emptiness at the very thought.

"What do you want for Christmas?" he asked suddenly.

"What?" She stopped the slow rubbing of her belly.

"I'm serious. What do you want? Chocolate? New embroidery thread?"

"Are you offering to get me something?" she asked with a smile on her lips.

"*Yah*, I am."

Her smiled slipped and she looked away. "I wish I could have a Christmas with my *daet*. I miss him…"

"Is he coming to see you?" Noah asked.

"No." Eve leaned her head back against the wooden wall. "This is a secret. I'm supposed to be helping some ailing family member, and my siblings don't even know what I'm really doing. If he comes to see me at Christmas, it will seem awfully strange to the ones at home, won't it? We have appearances to maintain."

"What do you want for Christmas?" he repeated quietly, and Eve turned to look at him. Her dark eyes sparkled in the low light, and she shook her head.

"I don't know," she whispered.

"I'm going to bring you something," he said.

"I don't have any money to get you anything," she said.

"I don't need presents," he replied, then he chuckled. "Maybe I'd ask for a Christmas kiss."

Her eyes sparkled with humor. "Now?"

Noah's heartbeat sped up, and he dropped his gaze. "If you're offering…"

Eve leaned toward him, her soft lips brushing his chilled cheek, and when she pulled back, he turned toward her again, and their eyes met. There was something in that moment that seemed to warm the space between them, and the teasing evaporated with their breath in the frigid air. A snowflake, blown through the cracks in the opposite wall, landed on a stray tendril of hair, balancing there, perfectly intact.

Noah reached forward and brushed the hair off her forehead, his hand touching her cold cheek, and she turned her face toward his touch, ever so subtly.

What was it about those pink lips, slightly parted, and the way her eyelashes touched her cheeks with each blink... When he leaned toward her, she leaned toward him, too, and their lips came together in a soft kiss.

Her breath was warm against his face, and it was like the storm, the shack, even the wood beneath them melted away, leaving them alone in this tender moment. He reached to pull her closer, but as he did, his hand brushed against her coat-clad belly and he felt a little movement from within—like something rolled against his touch.

He pulled back, and her eyes fluttered open. He didn't know what to say, and she put her hand over the spot he'd inadvertently touched.

"The baby's awake," she said, dropping her gaze.

He'd felt the baby move... He felt a rush of warmth at the thought—they weren't quite so alone as he'd been thinking, were they?

"I shouldn't have kissed you," he breathed.

"No, probably not," she agreed, looking up again. "All the same, it was very nice."

Noah smiled at that. "*Yah*. It was."

It was more than nice—it was intoxicating, healing, and it filled him with a yearning for more of the same, but he knew he was walking on thin ice already. What was he doing kissing the mother of Thomas and Patience's newest addition? If this felt wrong for him, how complicated must it be for her?

"We can't do this, though," she said, sucking in a breath.

"I know," he said quickly. "I'm very clear on that. I know it's wrong in all sorts of ways, I just..." He searched for the words to explain himself. "I don't go around kissing girls, you know."

"I'm glad... I think," she said, licking her lips.

"You're different," he said, his voice dropping. "You're strangely wise, and you're smart, and sweet and...beautiful. I've never met a girl quite like you."

"It doesn't matter," she said.

"I know."

"I'm leaving as soon as the baby comes, and—" Tears welled in her eyes.

"I know. I'm sorry—for all of it. I'm sorry you have to make this sacrifice, and that I'm connected to all of it, and..." He sighed. "I don't know what to say."

Noah reached out and took her gloved hand in his, wishing he could feel her soft skin next to his, instead of all this padding between them.

"We have to get back," Eve said.

She was right, of course, and he reached over from where he sat and pushed open the door. The wind had died down again, and they were left with softly falling snow once more.

Surfing through the trees, through the snow and over their mangled hearts, the sound of four-part harmony church singing reached them. It was a Christmas song— "It Came Upon a Midnight Clear"—and Noah's heart lifted with the words toward *Gott*.

Once, long ago, another baby was born to a vulnerable young mother... Noah had no business kissing

Eve, he knew that, but his feelings for her weren't just the kind of attraction that sparked between young men and women, either. This went deeper. He cared for her. And somehow that didn't make this easier.

"Let's get back," Noah agreed, and they both stood up and stepped back out into the gently falling snow.

Sometimes the arrival of a baby could bring both hope and heartbreak, and Noah could only pray that *Gott* would grant Eve's deepest hopes for that husband of her own. If Noah couldn't be the one to fill her heart, then she deserved a chance with another good man who would see the true treasure she was.

Chapter Nine

"That was a powerful sermon," *Mammi* said when they all came back from service late that afternoon. The snow had stopped falling, and the sun sparkled on the new white mantle that covered everything within sight.

"Yah," Noah said. "Very."

Noah looked out the window. There would be a fair amount of shoveling to do to make paths to the stable and to the little hay barn that held feed for the horses. Just because it was Sunday didn't mean the necessary work stopped.

"You know, I don't think we hear sermons on the role of men in our community often enough," *Mammi* said, taking off her good apron and replacing it with her kitchen one. Her swollen, knobby fingers worked slowly as she tied her apron behind her. "We hear about the sins we need to combat, and the beauty of marriage, and the important job of raising our *kinner* to honor *Gott*, but we don't hear about men specifically, do we? At least we haven't in a long time."

"Maybe not," Amos agreed. He crossed the kitchen

and picked up a muffin from a bowl on the counter. "It was certainly an engaging three hours."

Amos took a bite of the muffin, and *Mammi* took a plate from the cupboard and handed it to him. He accepted it with a rueful smile.

"And when the preacher said that men were put on this earth to protect and provide, I have to say, I felt a shiver," *Mammi* went on. "I've been blessed with strong, kind, patient men in my life. My own *daet*, my husband, my sons who grew up to be so much like their father, and now you boys taking care of me..."

Amos shot his grandmother a smile. "I'm grown, you know."

"Oh, you'll always be my boy, Amos," *Mammi* replied with a chuckle. Then she turned to Noah. "And I'm proud of how you've grown, too, Noah. You stood for what was right when your *mamm* left, and you never wavered."

Never wavered. Not that he'd admitted to, at least.

"I may have wavered a little," Noah said.

"Well, I never saw it," *Mammi* said. "And you're still that honorable young man I've grown so fond of."

She meant well, just loving them as she always had, but *Mammi*'s words cut deep. As a man in this community, it was his role to protect and provide, not to be toying with the emotions of a vulnerable woman who was in this community's care.

"Let's get out and start shoveling," Noah said to Amos. "I'd rather get it done in daylight."

"*Yah*, agreed," Amos replied, pushing the last of the muffin into his mouth.

He'd work—that might help purge his system of the growing guilt that he just couldn't seem to shake.

Noah didn't sleep well that night. He kept thinking of what a relief it had been to finally kiss Eve, which didn't help his guilt at all. It had been more than a kiss— it had been a connection at long last, and it felt like something inside his chest had been reaching toward her and was finally rewarded with a touch. Even remembering that kiss in the cold sped up his pulse. He'd never meant to feel more for her than gallant protectiveness, but somewhere—and he couldn't even tell when it had happened—his feelings had crossed that line.

What would his brother think if he knew what Noah was feeling for this woman? Noah was supposed to be helping Thomas and Patience, not muddling with their hopes of adopting the baby. He couldn't be tangling with Eve's emotions. She was supposed to be preparing to give her child to someone else…and he was kissing her? This was a betrayal to both his brother and to Eve. They were both counting on his strength of character to support them, not to be selfishly giving in to his own feelings.

Obviously, a relationship with her was impossible on too many levels, and he was playing with fire. Whatever this was *had* to stop. So he lay awake late that night praying for strength, for clarity, for whatever it would take to get him to stop tumbling down this emotional path.

Lord, convict me of how wrong that was, and forgive me for caving to my feelings. Make me into the man You created me to be, because I'm falling short. Pro-

tect Eve's heart, too. Bless her. Let me carry whatever
burden is right, but lighten hers...

He was still the man *Gott* had put in her path, and it
was his job to protect her, even now.

The next day, Noah was tired, but he got up early and
helped Amos with the chores before they headed off to
Redemption Carpentry together. By the time Thomas
arrived an hour later, Noah had already gotten most
of a side table stained. He looked up when his brother
came in. If his thoughtlessness had ruined this for his
brother, he wasn't going to forgive himself.

"You wouldn't believe how happy Patience is,"
Thomas said, pulling off his coat and hanging it on the
wall. He stomped his boots on the mat. "She's already
sewing a few little outfits."

"*Mammi* started crocheting a blanket the minute we
told her," Noah said. "The women will pull it all together. They always do."

Thomas pulled out the cradle, still a little rough, and
he squatted next to it.

"I've never been allowed to be a *daet* to a baby before," Thomas said quietly. "I won't know what to do."

"Patience will show you," Noah said.

"*Yah*, I guess." Thomas rose to his feet and shot Noah
a nervous smile. "You know when you've wanted something so badly and you finally get it... I'm half-afraid
it won't work out. Something will happen and she'll
choose someone else."

Noah dropped his gaze. He didn't need any fresh re-
minders about what he was toying with here.

"Don't worry about that," Amos said. "She and Patience have an agreement, don't they? This agreement was between women. It has very little to do with you."

Thomas cast Amos an annoyed look. "I'm going to be the father, Amos."

"*Yah*, and you'll have everything to do with the raising of that baby, but this agreement—" Amos paused. "That's what I'm talking about. Eve chose a mother. It's okay."

Hopefully Amos was right and her choice was about Patience, and Noah couldn't ruin it.

Noah stood up and brushed off his hands.

"I promised I'd bring the donations we've collected so far to Wollie's new place this morning," Noah said. "They're moving in today."

"That's great!" Amos said. "Give Wollie our best. It'll be nice to have him around again."

"Eve wanted to come along—see her cousin and all that," Noah added, and he wasn't sure why he was explaining himself, but he felt like he owed Amos and Thomas something, and he wasn't sure what.

"Sounds good," Amos replied. "Thomas and I had better stay and keep working on the orders, though."

"She's close to her due date," Thomas said.

"I'll keep a careful eye on her," Noah replied. "Maybe it will help distract her from…you know."

Thomas nodded, and there were a few beats of silence. It was a difficult topic to discuss, especially as men.

"Wollie and I can handle the lifting between us," Noah added, trying to sound cheerier than he felt. "But I'd better head out—moving day is always a little hectic."

"Right," Thomas replied, and the brothers exchanged a look. "Look after her for us."

Because right now, Thomas wasn't worrying about Wollie, he was thinking about the baby. And Noah couldn't blame him for that.

Today, Noah needed to keep his head about him—no more overstepping with Eve.

In fact, if he was going to be really honest, he owed Eve an apology.

Half an hour later, Noah had loaded the last of the donations onto the wagon, and he and Eve rattled down the road toward Wollie's new farmhouse. The day was warmer, hovering just below the freezing mark, and sunlight sparkled off last night's snow. As Noah and Eve left the town's limits, he noticed some deer footprints in the snow beside the road, and a blue jay flitted from post to post along the barbed-wire fence that ran alongside them. It was a perfect winter morning, or it would have been if he didn't feel like he'd let everyone down.

"How are you feeling?" Noah asked.

Eve glanced toward him. "Fine. Everyone keeps asking that." She shrugged. "But I feel no different than I did yesterday. The baby isn't showing any signs of arriving today, at least."

"Okay," he said. "Um. That's good. I was a bit worried after yesterday."

Eve cast him an understanding smile. "It's okay. I'll be fine."

"No, I mean—" Noah had to get this out. "Look, I overstepped—by a lot. I shouldn't have asked you for that kiss—I shouldn't have kissed you, period. And I'm sorry."

"I'm okay," she said quietly.

"I know you're dealing with a lot right now," he said. "I'm adding more complication to your life, and that's wrong of me. That sermon yesterday was awfully convicting. I wasn't being the man I should have been."

Eve looked over at him, her gaze meeting his for a moment, then flickering down to her gloved hands that were resting on top of her belly.

"Do you know what it's like to be pregnant and never have been kissed before?" she asked.

Noah's heart stuttered, and he saw some pink rise in her cheeks.

"No?" He hadn't meant for it to sound like a question, but it had caught him off guard.

"I spent my time with my *mamm*," she went on, "helping her to feel more comfortable, going with her to doctor's appointments, taking care of the housework and the cooking." Eve sighed. "And being so busy with my *mamm*, I wasn't getting to know the boys, going to young people's events, or that sort of thing. I hadn't been out to a hymn sing in ages. That might just be my excuse for not having anyone interested in taking me home from singing, but I didn't have any boys who came calling. That's what I'm trying to say."

Was she saying what he thought she was saying… had he taken more from her than he'd imagined?

"So when I kissed you—" he said, his voice catching.

"It was my first kiss." She raised her gaze to meet his again.

"I feel worse," he breathed.

"Don't feel bad," she said with a sad flicker of a smile. "Like I said, I'm pregnant, and up until yesterday, I didn't know what it felt like to be kissed. And I'm actually grateful to know—especially with someone who seems like he genuinely cares."

"I do care," he said earnestly. "I'm not the kind of man who just... I'm not that kind of man. So I care more than I should. You're quite incredible, you know."

"I think there is something about pregnancy that makes a girl seem like more than she really is," Eve said. "More wicked, perhaps. Or wiser. Or sweeter. I don't know. But I'm still just Eve Schrock, a farmer's daughter who didn't steer clear of that Englisher party."

"Your last name is Schrock?" he asked quietly.

"*Yah.* I'd appreciate you not telling people, though. It doesn't help in keeping secrets."

But she'd trusted *him*, and that tugged at him all the same.

"I don't blame you for that party," he said quietly.

"That's nice," she said. "I do appreciate that. But blame me or not, I still have to live with the consequences, don't I?"

The horses plodded along, and a chill wind blew snow up from the field in a white haze. Noah put his head down against the icy blast, and he reached out to tug Eve a little closer against his side. While she was here, he'd protect her.

"You're going to find a good man," Noah said. "And you'll get that family you want so much. I know it."

"I hope so," she replied.

If Eve could see herself the way he saw her, she'd be a lot more confident in that. She might not have been courted yet back in her hometown, wherever that was, but he had no doubt that when she returned, more than one single man would take notice. She had a certain glow about her, a gentleness, a depth, that Noah hadn't seen before in any other woman. It was drawing him in, too.

"Noah, how come *you* aren't married yet?" Eve asked.

"Me?" Noah laughed self-consciously. "I'm tough to tie down, I guess."

"That's it?" she asked.

Noah sighed. She'd opened up to him, after all. "I have a hard time trusting myself—my ability to choose the right woman. When everything you believed to be true ends up being wrong, it makes it hard to trust your own instincts anymore."

"But your faith wasn't wrong," she said. "Right and wrong doesn't change. You stayed to the narrow path, and that was a good choice."

"My parents weren't what I thought they were, though," he said. "They'd held back a lot, and I guess I'm afraid that if they could hold back that much and keep me oblivious, then anyone could. I'm…less trusting now." He hadn't admitted that before, and he looked down at Eve apologetically. "I don't mean to keep dumping my problems on you, you know."

"I like to hear it," she said. "For what it's worth, I think you should get married. You'd make a good husband."

Noah felt his face heat, and he chuckled self-consciously. *"Yah?"*

"Yah." But there was no teasing in her voice, and when he met her level gaze, the part of him that was supposed to stay resolute trembled just a little.

If only it were that easy to marry. A man couldn't

always have everything—his community, his faith and the woman he was most powerfully drawn to. And it was going to be harder to settle down after Eve left, not easier. No one else would be Eve.

They came to a corner, and Noah guided the horses around it. He could see the farmhouse from here—a green SUV parked out front, and some *kinner* running and playing in the snow of the front yard.

"I think that's Wollie's family," Noah said.

Eve leaned forward and shaded her eyes. Wollie waved his hand overhead, and the woman turned and looked in their direction, too.

Wollie and Natasha needed the basics this Christmas—furniture, bedding, clothes. One disaster had served as a reminder of what was really important, and that wasn't an extravagant Christmas.

Noah's Christmas needs weren't extravagant, either. He needed to put these complex feelings for Eve in the background and be the man he knew he needed to be. With *Gott*'s help.

Eve couldn't help but notice how strong Noah was, easily hoisting heavy boxes, carrying them into the house and stacking them in the empty, echoing living room. The men's boots thunked against the linoleum floor, little Caleb tramping along after them, carrying lighter items, and the youngest boy, Cory, following along just for the fun of it.

Eve sat at the newly set up kitchen table—a recent donation—her baby shifting around inside her as if trying to get more comfortable. The baby wouldn't set-tle, no matter how much Eve rubbed her belly, maybe reacting to her discomfort. Sitting in a kitchen with an Englisher woman was disconcerting.

Natasha wore close-fitting jeans and had her hair pulled back into a ponytail that drew Eve's gaze. Natasha's parenting style was very different, too—letting the girls do whatever amused them, and when they were naughty, Natasha just rolled her eyes.

"I haven't met much of Wollie's family or old friends," Natasha said, sitting down at the kitchen table opposite Eve. "But Wollie has talked about Noah before—they used to swim together in a creek. Did you know that?" She smiled. "Wollie has the best childhood memories."

There was no tea to share—but there was a box of cookies that Eve had thought to bring, and a larger box of baked goods sitting on the kitchen counter behind them. The Zooks would need some food before they stocked up at a grocery store. Natasha's gaze moved over to where her four-year-old daughter was eating a cookie over a heating vent that was blowing some welcome warm air. The toddler crouched next to her older sister, her fair hair fluttering in the warm blast.

"You're Wollie's cousin, right?" Natasha asked.

"*Yah*. Distant, but we're related. He came to help my *daet* with the corn shocks one year, and we got to know him better."

"The corn shocks?" Natasha asked.

"It's…farming stuff." Eve smiled and shrugged. "But family is family—*Gott* put us all together for a reason. That's what we believe."

Natasha nodded a couple of times. "I'm not close with my extended family. We had a few family reunions when I was a kid, but we've all drifted since my grandmother passed."

"So you don't go visit anyone?" Eve asked.

"Not really." Natasha shrugged. "We don't have much in common, honestly."

Being part of the same family seemed like a rather large thing to have in common. It was sad to think of a family so distant as to not get together anymore. Amish families made a point of gathering as often as possible. What was life without family ties?

"I'm sure you'll see more of his family, living out there," Eve said.

"Maybe. We'll see," Natasha replied noncommittally. "The thing is, marrying me was a big deal, you know? They're still pretty miffed."

"*Yah*, I could see that," Eve replied.

"Can you?" Natasha frowned. "What's the big deal? We're married! We have kids. We're a family—"

"He has more family than just you, though," Eve said, then sighed and softened her voice. "His parents love him just as much as you love your own little ones."

"I met them a couple of times, but they've never been warm," she replied. "That's all I'm saying. They disapprove, and after four children together, we no longer care."

And what did Eve know about the tensions within Wollie's family? Maybe Natasha was right about her in-laws' attitudes. Still, there was something in the woman's voice that suggested she cared more than she said.

"Besides," Natasha went on, "I don't think I could ever do all the things you Amish women do—cooking from scratch, sewing your own clothes, going without a microwave! I mean—I couldn't do it!"

"Why not?" Eve asked.

"It's—" Natasha met Eve's gaze. "It's terrifying. Wollie tells me about his mother's cooking, and how they'd gather around the stove in the winter, and all these stories that sound so simple and wonderful, like *Little House on the Prairie* come back to life, but he didn't marry me because I could provide that. He married me because I was different."

"I'm not married," Eve said. "So I have no advice on how things are between a husband and a wife, but I can say this… We Amish believe that Christianity isn't about one person's talents or abilities—it's about what we are together as a community. And there are plenty of women who would be happy to show you how to start a garden, and how to sew some clothes, and give you some recipes to try out. Wollie's one of us, and like it or not, you're connected to us, too, now. But you don't have to do any of it alone."

The men came back inside just then with more boxes, and the little girls came running to meet them, nearly tripping them in their excitement.

"Careful now," Wollie said, scooping up his smaller daughter in one arm. "Go on over to your *mamm*."

Eve noticed how Natasha's expression softened at the Dutch word. There was more Amish in her home than she seemed to realize.

"You really think they'd help me figure it out if I wanted to…try?" Natasha asked, turning back to Eve.

"*Yah*, I do," Eve replied. "In fact, Noah's *mamm* was born English, too. I imagine she'd be a big help."

"I'm not sure they're as accepting as you're making out," Natasha said. "You're here to give up your baby—because they aren't so accepting of differences. Right?"

Eve looked away, and her heart squeezed. How could she explain herself to an outsider? This woman wouldn't understand—Englishers never did. They just judged.

"I want to get married," Eve said quietly. "And if I'm a single mother, that won't happen easily. I'd still be part of the community, I'd just…miss out on the things I've longed for all my life." She paused. "And I love our lifestyle. I love how we women pull together and make quilts or bake pies. We women make a home, and I love how the men take care of the farming and the men's work. It's satisfying to do our jobs well…and I love how our Plain life gives us the chance to focus on the things that matter most—loving *Gott*, supporting each other and the raising of *kinner*—children, I mean. I like the cozy warmth of a fire in a woodstove, and the soft light of a kerosene lamp hung over a kitchen table on a winter evening. But more than anything, I want little ones to look at me and call me *mamm* without my reputation being a burden to them. I want a houseful of children of my own, and I want a husband to love, like you have. I want a man to come home to me, to eat my cooking and to hold me close. I love our Plain life so much that I'm willing to make this sacrifice so that both me and my child can have *everything* an Amish life offers."

Natasha was silent for a moment, then she nodded. "It sounds beautiful. I'm sorry it comes at such a price for you."

"We're conservative people," Eve said. "And if you

don't like that, you won't like living the Amish life. But that also means that my child would have a fuller, better life with an already established family. It's not perfect, but it's the life I've been raised to love. And I can't think of a better life to give this baby. That's how much I believe in our faith, and our way of living. It's not just words for me."

Natasha nodded. "I can see that."

But more than being a beautiful experience of the simple things, a Plain life meant commitment. It meant giving up conveniences for the deeper beauty of work and family. And that kind of commitment could only be made *as* a family.

The men came back in with the last of the donations from the wagon, and after some polite talking, it was time for Noah and Eve to take their leave. Once they'd said their goodbyes and Eve was settled back up on the wagon seat once more, Natasha came outside, her feet thrust into her husband's boots, and no coat over her sweater. She came up to the side of the wagon.

"Here," Natasha said, handing her something covered in a napkin. Eve peeked inside. It was an apple turnover. "I know what it's like to be pregnant, and I'm always hungry when I am! You'd better bring a snack." She paused. "And thank you—for the food, for the donations... And for the visit. I'm grateful."

Eve met the other woman's gaze, and in that moment, it wasn't about Amish and English anymore. It was about two women who might understand each other just a little bit better now. Eve felt her eyes mist.

"Thank you," she said, and Noah flicked the reins.

"Merry Christmas!" Noah called, and Natasha

stepped back, crossing her arms against the cold as Wollie put an arm around her shoulders.

It was strange to be envious of an Englisher, but Eve was. No matter if Natasha realized it or not, she had something wonderful in a husband and a houseful of children. And they might have been reduced to the bare essentials with that fire, but the Zooks were within a whisper of an Amish life, forced upon them. Sometimes the greatest blessings came like that—without a lot of choice. All the same, Natasha had a man to eat her cooking—that was a gift from *Gott*. While He was blessing others, Eve could only pray that He wouldn't forget her.

Noah guided the horses back up the drive as they headed toward town once more. They rode in silence for a few minutes, and Eve took a bite of the sweet, flaky turnover. Aunt Lovina's baking was superb, as always.

"We might see Wollie for Christmas," Noah said. "I suggested he join us, and he said he'd try. We'll see."

"Your *mamm* could be a real help to her," Eve said, but as she said it, a low ache spread across her belly. Eve leaned forward, looking for a more comfortable position.

"Are you okay?" Noah asked.

"*Yah...*" She put the pastry on the seat between them and shifted again. "I'm just a little uncomfortable."

"Should I stop?" he asked.

She shook her head. "No, no, I'm fine. I was thinking that your *mamm* might be able to show Natasha some plain cooking...some sewing? She's intimidated by the work, but if Wollie wants to come back, he can't do that alone."

Noah flicked the reins to get the horses going a little bit faster, and Eve shut her eyes against the strange ache. This wasn't labor, was it? It couldn't be. If she was in labor, she'd know it! That's what she'd been told by every other woman who had given her advice.

"I'm sure *Mamm* would be happy to show her a few things," Noah replied. "But doesn't having another Englisher around bother you?"

Eve adjusted her position again. "How else do we bring Wollie back? He can't do it without his wife—" She winced.

"You're not okay," Noah said curtly, and when he reached out to take her hand, she let out a slow breath and squeezed his hand.

"Maybe we could pick up the pace a little bit," she admitted, and blew out a slow breath.

Maybe it was just that she'd been in a wagon too long and could use some rest, but she needed to get back to the fabric shop. Lovina would know what to do.

Chapter Ten

When Noah reined the horses to a stop in front of Quilts and Such, a line of cars stopped behind them, and Noah irritably waved them to pass. One by one the cars crept by, keeping him from getting down, and he felt a surge of frustration. Another car slowed, and he gestured for it to go past.

"Go!" he said out loud. "For crying out loud, just go!"

The Englishers in the car looked at him with wide, curious eyes, and he didn't have the patience for them right now. Eve was in labor—or she was in trouble. But he'd been watching her as she rubbed her hand over her belly and leaned forward. She was utterly silent except for the rush of an exhaled breath.

A little group of carolers walked down the sidewalk, singing "Away in a Manger," and a few pirouetting snowflakes drifted from the sky. Had he been a fool to even bring her along to see Wollie's family? She'd been anxious to see her cousin, but a long wagon ride on snowy roads might have been really stupid on his part.

"Let me help you get down," Noah said, as the last

car passed and he jumped to the ground on his side. He circled around, past the horses and their clouds of exhaled breath, and he held up his hands to help her. But she grimaced and leaned forward again.

"Is everything okay?" Lovina's voice came from the front door of Quilts and Such, and Noah looked over to see Eve's aunt pulling a shawl around her shoulders. She bustled up and looked at Eve, then exchanged a look with Noah.

"She's pretty uncomfortable," Noah said. "I'm not sure what that means."

"When did this start?" Lovina asked briskly.

"About three miles back," Noah replied, and Lovina rolled her eyes.

"Time, Noah, not distance!" she snapped, and he felt foolish.

"Uh—twenty minutes ago?" he said.

"We have time, then," Lovina said with a nod. "Eve, how are you feeling now?"

"It's getting better," Eve replied. "It's not so bad now. This might be nothing. Maybe just too must jostling, you know?"

"I'm glad you're feeling a little better," Lovina said, and when Eve made a move to try to get down, she shook her head. "No, dear. Noah, I need you to drive Eve back to our place, and I'm going to go fetch the midwife."

Finally—something he could do. Noah nodded. "Of course. I'll get right to it."

"It could be nothing," Eve said, but even as the words came out, she grimaced again.

"Maybe so, but better safe than sorry," Lovina said,

and she pulled out a key and passed it over to Noah. "That will get you into the house. I don't think anyone is home right now. Come on. *Schnell!* Let's get moving! I've got the girls to watch the shop for me, so no harm if this is a false alarm, Eve. But I suggest we treat it like it's the real thing, okay?" Eve leaned back against the seat, and Lovina put a hand on Noah's coat sleeve. "Don't leave her alone. You stay with her until I'm back, you hear me?"

"*Yah.* I'll stay," he said.

"Good." Lovina gave a curt nod. "And once you get there, if she's uncomfortable, you could walk with her a little. That tends to help."

"Okay." Noah swallowed, and he headed back around to get up into the wagon again. Once there, he put his arm around Eve and pulled her closer against his side. He wasn't trying to do anything inappropriate, but he wanted to make sure that if he had to catch her, he'd be close enough to do it. She leaned against him, and he felt better.

The ride back to the Glick house seemed like an eternity, and Eve leaned against him as he guided the horses down the familiar streets, reining them in at stop signs and waiting on the Englisher traffic. It was a strange relief to be able to be the strong body next to her, to let her press into his shoulder as he flicked the reins and urged the horses on again. He didn't even care who saw them—there were bigger concerns right now.

When they got back to the Glick house, Noah pulled the wagon up close, then hopped down first. He helped Eve down, and she all but fell into his arms as another pain hit her. She leaned forward and moaned.

"Eve, let's get inside," he said. "Your aunt says walking might help."

"Yah..." She straightened. "I don't think I'm ready for this..."

"For what?" he asked feebly.

"For having a baby!" Tears welled in her eyes. "I don't think I can do this!"

Noah had nothing to say to that—this was the women's realm, and he didn't know one thing about childbirth.

"With me here, sure, you feel like it's impossible," he said. "But I'm just a man! When your aunt and the midwife come, they'll take over."

"True..." She smiled faintly, and they walked together toward the door—Noah with his arm around her waist lest she slip, and he caught a handful of her coat, just to be sure. He fiddled with the key, but managed to unlock the door, then he helped her inside.

"Come on," he said. "You sit down, and I'll get a fire started in the stove to warm it up in here."

The natural gas furnace kept the house at a livable temperature, but real comfort came from a woodstove. Noah swung the door shut and helped Eve to step out of her boots, then he peeled off his own coat and boots and headed into the kitchen to get started.

It felt strange to be taking charge in someone else's home like this, but it didn't take him long to locate the wood and kindling, then get a fire started in the cold belly of the black stove. Eve didn't sit, though. She paced back and forth through the kitchen, one hand on the small of her back as she walked.

"Your aunt wants me to stay until she gets here,"

Noah said, standing up and closing the stove's door as a fire took hold inside. "I hope you don't mind."

"Noah, I *want* you to stay," she said with a faint laugh. "Maybe you can distract me—"

"How?" he asked.

"Tell me about you and Wollie when you were *kinner*," she said. "Natasha said there are stories about the two of you…"

"Oh, *yah*," Noah said with a chuckle. "I'm not sure which of us was the bad influence, but there are stories!"

"So tell me one," she said.

Noah thought back to those childhood years. "Well, there was the time Wollie and I snuck up on Wollie's older sister when she was sitting in a buggy outside his house with her boyfriend. Thomas and I were sleeping over that night because *Mamm* and *Daet* were helping with some community emergency that I can't remember. But us three boys, we snuck outside and made wild animal sounds, hoping to scare his sister and her boyfriend."

"Did it work?" Eve stopped by the stove and put her hand out toward the heat, exhaling slowly. He could tell she was still in pain.

"*Yah*. It worked, but it had also interrupted a proposal." Noah glanced toward the door, wondering how long Lovina would take. "We were forgiven, but only because Wollie's parents were too excited about planning that wedding—that was the longest courtship ever, and everyone was antsy to get things moving forward for those two. So they forgot about punishing us boys in all the excitement."

"Was that Waneta's wedding?" Eve asked, meeting his gaze. "Wollie's sister?"

"*Yah*—Waneta and John. They've got eleven *kinner* now, I believe. They moved away, though."

Eve dropped her gaze, pressing her lips together, and Noah reached out and caught her hand. Her grip was tight and iron-strong, and Noah watched her face as she paled, her nostrils flaring.

"Eve—" He didn't know how to help her, how to make any of this easier.

"I want that..." she whispered.

"Three boys to punish?" he asked, attempting to joke.

"A proposal," she said, her grip on his hand loosening once more, and she let go of him. "I want annoying younger family members, and meddling in-laws, a proposal from a good man and a wedding with as much celery soup as the community can eat." She blew out another slow breath. "If I can manage it."

"You'll manage it," he said. "Trust me on that."

Eve ran her hand over her belly, then she wiped some hair back from her face that had fallen loose from her *kapp*. Tears misted her eyes.

"But more than my own happiness, I want my child to have a happy childhood like we had—getting into trouble, building friendships, learning to sit still on Service Sunday, and all without the burden of a *mamm* who got pregnant outside of marriage."

Noah nodded. "Thomas and Patience will love that baby well—I can guarantee that."

Eve turned away from him. "If you'd known your parents were converts when you were young—if everyone else had known—would it have changed things for you, do you think?"

He wouldn't have felt quite so comfortable in his life. He would have wondered about the Englisher side of the family, and he might not have felt quite so free to make mistakes and learn alongside the other boys. He would have known he was different...

"Yah," he was forced to admit. "It would have."

She nodded. "I thought so..."

Eve leaned forward again and closed her eyes. He grabbed a chair from the table and pulled it over, then helped her to sit down in front of the stove. She let out a shaky breath.

"Noah," she whispered.

"Yah?" He leaned closer.

"I'm having a baby today, and I know for a fact that I'm not ready." Her chin trembled.

"I think you're more ready than you realize," he whispered back. "You're strong, Eve. And *Gott* isn't letting you go—"

Outside he heard the clop of hooves and the crunch of wagon wheels, and he felt a surge of relief. That would be her aunt returning with the midwife.

Whatever he could do for Eve wasn't nearly what she needed! And the women who could take over and get her safely through this ordeal had arrived.

Gott, *take care of her...please.*

The door opened and Lovina came inside, another woman behind her. Eve looked up to see a competent-looking older woman, about Lovina's age by appearances, pulling her gloves off and stepping out of her boots in an efficient sort of way. She tossed her gloves onto the table and gave Eve a reassuring smile.

"Eve," she said. "My name is Sarah, and I'm the midwife. How are you doing?"

"I'm—" Eve shook her head. "I have no idea!"

"Are you still feeling contractions?" Sarah asked.

"I think so—it hurts."

Sarah's gaze whisked over to Noah. "Not the father...?"

Apparently, the midwife had been informed about the delicacy of the situation, and Lovina met Eve's gaze and she lifted her shoulders faintly. The fewer people who knew right now, the easier it would be for Eve to go back to her home and not have any telling rumors left to follow her back.

"Not the father," Noah said, his strong voice echoing through the kitchen, and Eve felt a sudden wave of panic. She was about to have a baby, and the man who was standing by her and giving her strength was the brother of the man who'd adopt this child... He wasn't really anything to her—nothing she could claim, at least.

"Then we need you out," Sarah said, her tone having the matter-of-fact timbre of a schoolteacher's. "In fact, if you'd be so kind as to stable the horses so that Lovina and I can get to work here, that would be much appreciated."

"*Yah*. Of course." Noah took a step toward the door, then he looked back at Eve, his eyes filled with sadness, worry and something else she couldn't quite name, but it made her own heart squeeze in response.

"Out!" Sarah said, gesturing toward the door. "I need

to check on my little mother, and I can't do that with you here."

Noah nodded quickly and walked briskly toward the door. In a moment, his coat and boots were back on and the door banged shut behind him, leaving the women alone. As soon as he was gone, the feeling of the room immediately changed. It was time to get down to business.

"Now, Eve," Sarah said. "You're scared to death—I can see it. And every first-time mother I've ever helped has felt the exact same way. But don't you worry—this is the hard part, and soon enough it will be over."

"I am scared," Eve said.

"Every single one of us arrived into this world the exact same way," Sarah said. "And then our *mamms* went on to do it again seven or eight more times! This is the way *Gott* has ordained it, and while it's hard, it's a system that works. I can promise you that."

Eve looked toward her aunt, uncertain of what she was even hoping for. Eve was more than frightened of the delivery—she was dreading the moment afterward when she'd see this child and fall in love even more than she already had.

"All right. This is the hard part, but soon enough you'll be able to start the healing. And it will get better. I do promise that, Eve. It will get better…but right now, we're going to be with you, and we'll get you through this, okay?"

How many times had this midwife seen a similar situation when a baby was born and handed off to another family? Was this more common than Eve liked to think? Somehow, this woman's brisk, reassuring way of facing all of it was just what she needed.

"You'll be fine, dear," Lovina said. "Now, I'm going to start some water boiling, and I'll fetch some towels. I'm thinking we need to get you upstairs."

"Yes, we need a bed," Sarah agreed. "But let's get her up and walking first. If she can still talk, this isn't active labor yet."

Eve allowed Sarah to help her to her feet, and as she rose, she was able to see out the side window. Noah was just leading the horses into the stable, and he looked over his shoulder as he passed, his gaze locking on to hers for a split second before Sarah's solid presence blocked her view. He was still here... Why did that comfort her?

If *Gott* blessed her, the next time she gave birth, there would be a husband by her side, and a husband wouldn't be chased out. He'd be proud and happy, and when she delivered that child, it would stay in her arms.

By the time Noah was heading back out with the wagon, it was past closing time at the shop, so instead of going toward town, he turned the horses in the direction of home. He had to tell his brother that Eve was in labor, and everyone would be happy and anxious. They'd all be praying for a safe delivery, but Thomas and Patience would be praying for something more—an addition to their family.

But Noah's prayers went deeper still. He was praying for Eve, for her safety and for her heart, because he knew how horrifically difficult this was going to be for her. Eve loved this baby, and it was only out of the deepest love that she could consider giving it up.

Noah roused himself as they approached the acreage Thomas and Patience shared with *Mamm*. He was the bearer of exciting news, but he couldn't bring himself to feel happy about it.

When he reined the horses in, he saw his mother in the window, looking out at him past the curtain. She smiled and raised a hand. Was it the look on his face that made her seem hesitant, or was it that they'd had so much tension between them the last few years that it was hard to overcome, even at Christmas?

He suddenly felt very tired, and as he got himself down from the wagon, he looked over at the smudge of red that still glowed on the western horizon. For Noah, this was going to be another difficult Christmas, but that was nothing compared to what Eve would endure.

The side door opened and his mother gave him a smile.

"Hello, son!" she called, and Rue appeared behind her skirts.

"Hi, Uncle Noah!" Rue called.

"Are you coming for dinner?" Rachel asked. "Because we have plenty!"

Noah came inside, and Patience smiled at him from the stove where she was stirring a pot of what smelled like chicken stew.

"We do have plenty," Patience confirmed. "It's good to see you, Noah."

"*Mammi* is teaching me to knit, and I'm going to make Toby a sweater!" Rue said, hopping from foot to foot.

"Chickens don't wear sweaters," he said with a chuckle.

"Toby will! And it's going to keep him cozy warm all winter long!"

"I think the hens will keep him warm," he said. "And the chicken house. Sometimes, your *daet* will even put a heater out there."

"But it's a Christmas sweater," Rue replied stubbornly. "I just don't know how to make the arms."

Rue wasn't going to be sidetracked from her mission it seemed, and Noah just laughed, then looked up to meet his sister-in-law's gaze.

"I came by because Eve has gone into labor," he said in Dutch so that his niece wouldn't understand.

"She has!" Patience dropped the spoon onto the stove top with a clatter.

"How long has it been?" Rachel asked.

"A couple of hours?" he replied.

Both women relaxed.

"It'll be a while, then," Rachel replied. "It takes longer than that."

"Do we tell Rue?" Patience said, more to herself than to the rest of them.

"Tell me what?" Rue asked.

"You understood that, did you?" Patience chuckled, switching to English. "Nothing, sugar. I'm just thinking out loud."

"Even if she has the baby in the night, she deserves to hold her child until morning," Rachel said softly in Dutch, and she and Patience exchanged a sad look.

"Yah," Patience said quietly. "She does. Going over

there in the morning is soon enough. Tonight, we should pray for *Gott*'s will."

"Rue and I have been getting some toys together to bring to Wollie's *kinner* for Christmas," Rachel said, switching to English again for the girl's benefit. "We've found some very nice toys, haven't we?"

"*Yah*, and we've got some from the neighbor kids, too!" Rue announced proudly.

"We can bring those to Wollie's family tomorrow morning—just you and me." Rachel bent down with a smile. "Those poor *kinner* have lost all their toys in that fire. And they don't have chickens to play with. But I think they'll be so happy to have the toys we've collected."

"Just us?" Rue whispered delightedly, then she turned to Patience. "Can we, *Mamm*? Can we go bring presents to those Englisher kids with no chickens?"

Patience nodded. "Yes, of course. That's what Christmas is all about."

"Those *kinner* need a chicken, Uncle Noah," Rue said, and he could see her little brain starting to glow with this new idea. "Think how happy they'd be with a Christmas chicken!"

Noah smothered a grin. "Will it make their *mamm* happy, though?"

"How could it not?" Rue asked earnestly.

Noah rubbed a hand over his chin and tried not to smile as he considered the fallout of his niece's grand idea.

"Now, come eat with us," Rachel said, turning to give Noah a hopeful smile. "*Mammi* Mary gets to feed you more often than we do, and I miss my son."

And just like that, everything was arranged. Rue would be off with her grandmother, bringing gifts to the Zook home, which would free up Thomas and Patience to go meet their new baby on the morning of Christmas Eve.

This would be a very happy Christmas for Thomas's home—they'd have a new baby to cuddle and love, and they'd be filled with thankfulness. For this home, at least. Not for Eve.

A buggy rattled up the drive, and Rue hopped back over to the window.

"*Daet*'s home!" she said excitedly. "And I'm going to tell him about Toby's new sweater!"

Thomas, no doubt, would be less than thrilled at the thought of dressing up that scruffy rooster. Someone would have to tell her that it wasn't a possibility, but Noah wasn't going to be the bad guy this evening. A new baby in the home would be enough to distract her later on. Hopefully.

"I suppose I'll stay for supper, then," Noah said, casting his sister-in-law a smile. "But let me go out and take care of the horses."

Because no matter what excitement was in the air, no matter what change was on the horizon, there was still work to be done. It kept their boots on the ground and their hearts humble.

As he headed back out into the winter chill, he prayed that *Gott* would help him to get his head level again… because Eve wasn't his to worry over. His heart didn't belong in the middle of this baby's birth. This was Thomas and Patience's baby—and they deserved to celebrate.

Chapter Eleven

At one o'clock in the morning on Christmas Eve, while snow swirled outside the window and wind howled around the house, Eve gave birth to a healthy baby boy. He let out a powerful cry after his first breath, and when Sarah wrapped him in a blanket and laid him in Eve's arms, she looked down at that tiny, squished face and her heart cracked in two.

They said that when a baby was born, so was a mother, and Eve had wondered if it would be different for her, because she would never raise this child, but it wasn't. She felt herself change and grow, and turn inside out, if that were even possible, all in a single moment looking down at the baby in her arms.

And yet this transformation would have to remain a secret, and the growth of her heart, swelling to encompass the child, no matter how far away he might go, would be something she could never speak of.

Snow whipped against the windowpane, but the room was warm and cozy as Sarah and Lovina rushed about cleaning things up and carrying towels and basins of water back out of the room again. Eve looked at the baby, and tears trickled down her cheeks.

"I love you," she whispered. "I will always love you. I promise you that…always…"

She didn't want her aunt to hear her—or Sarah. Somehow it felt like showing weakness to let them see this moment between her and her child. Everyone knew that this baby boy would be raised a Wiebe.

Eve had wondered what this baby would look like, this baby that had been forced upon her, that she had not chosen. Would he have an Englisher look about him— whatever that might mean? But he didn't. He looked perfectly innocent, with a shock of black hair that stood straight up, tiny rosebud lips, and a face that looked positively boyish. Whatever trauma had surrounded his conception, he was a beautiful baby.

When he squirmed, she'd talk softly to him, and he'd settle immediately, just like he used to do when he was inside her and she'd rub her hand over her belly. It was like there was something inside him that told him he belonged to her, some physical connection that still lingered…and yet he'd have to learn a different voice and a different touch to trust soon enough.

"You need rest, Eve," Lovina said softly, opening the bedroom door again.

"I'm okay," Eve said.

"A woman needs to recover," Lovina said. "You've gone through a very big ordeal tonight, and you need to let us take care of you."

"I said I'm okay!" Eve's voice strengthened. "I'm not putting him down yet."

"We could put a little cradle next to the bed—" Lovina started.

"No!"

She wouldn't give up a single moment with him— their time together was short enough as it was. There would be time to sleep and grieve and heal... But that time was not now.

Lovina retreated once more, and she could hear the murmur of voices in the hallway. Her cousins, the midwife...and her uncle? Yes, that was who it was, and Eve didn't care. She was taking over a whole room, and she didn't care. For this one night she was going to be selfish and hold her baby.

The baby opened his mouth in a yawn, and she touched his tiny chin with the tip of her finger. Eve knew what she'd name him if she could—Samuel. Because she felt like Hannah having to give up her child, though he would never be out of *Gott*'s care. But it wasn't her place to name this child—his adoptive parents would do that. Her only job was to find a way to let go.

Eve did her best to stay awake that night, although she did doze, but she wouldn't let anyone take the baby from her arms. She'd hand him to one woman—and only when she had to.

Gott, *protect my son*, she prayed, leaning her head back against the cool pillow. *Provide for him, bless him, and as he grows up, show him how very real You are! And please, if You could impress upon his little heart one more thing—let him always know with absolute certainty that his* mamm *loved him...and that I did my best.*

Tears leaked from the corners of her eyes, and she let out a shuddering sigh. She didn't want to sleep—she wanted to stay awake and memorize every detail of her son's face and fingers and the way he breathed... She wanted to know that if she saw him again in a crowd, even after years and years, that she'd recognize him. A mother should recognize her child anywhere—it was only right... But she was so very tired, and before she knew it, she'd drifted into an unsettled sleep.

Eve woke up three more times that night to feed the baby and to change his diaper. Lovina helped her with those things—the midwife having left, and her cousins sleeping in another room. Wordlessly, they'd given the baby his bottle, let him drain it, and then changed that wee diaper so that he'd be dry and comfortable, but Eve wouldn't let him be put into the cradle that had materialized next to the bed.

When Eve awoke the last time, there was daylight flooding into the bedroom—the snow from last night had passed, and sunlight sparkled on the snow collected outside the window. She looked down at the baby in her arms, heard voices downstairs, and her heart sped up. She knew who was here—it was Patience and Thomas come to collect their baby. Her mouth went dry, and she pulled the infant closer against her as she heard the footsteps coming up the stairs. Her door opened and Lovina came in first.

"They're here," she said simply.

Eve nodded, and Patience and Thomas came inside, too, the little bedroom suddenly feeling very full. Eve lay on the bed, her arms aching from staying in the same position for so long, but she wouldn't give herself a break. She didn't dare—she'd only regret it later when she tried to remember what he felt like in her arms, and she wouldn't cheat herself of one second with her baby.

"How are you doing?" Patience asked, pulling up a chair next to the bed and sinking into it.

"I'm all right," Eve said.

"Are you in much pain?" Patience asked.

"Some," Eve admitted. "That's to be expected, I suppose."

Patience leaned forward and nudged the blanket away from the baby's face, and a smile tickled her lips.

"He's beautiful, Eve," Patience breathed.

"Yah, I know..." Tears welled in her eyes. "He's the most beautiful baby I've ever seen, and I've seen many."

"How much does he weigh?" Patience asked.

"Eight pounds, nine ounces," Lovina said. "And nineteen inches long. He's very healthy, Sarah says."

"Yah..." Patience said with a weak smile.

Would Eve forget those details over time? They just felt like numbers right now, swimming in a deeper, more important moment. She might not remember his weight, she realized, but she would remember the way his eyelashes touched his cheeks when he slept, and how his little lips sucked, as if he were dreaming of milk.

"Would you give us a moment?" Patience asked, turning to look at Lovina and Thomas. "I think that Eve and I could use a little privacy for this..."

They both hesitated, but when Patience met her husband's gaze, he nodded. Thomas and Lovina left the room and shut the door behind them, leaving Patience and Eve alone with the baby.

"They were looming," Patience said with a weak shrug.

"They were," Eve agreed.

"Do you still want to do this?" Patience asked. "Have you changed your mind?"

Eve had asked herself that question a thousand times since she'd first held her son, but while it was going to be an agonizing parting, she knew it was best for him. He needed a proper Amish family, so he could have a happy, carefree life. Keeping him would be selfish, she'd decided. What could she give him but a legacy of shame?

"No, I haven't changed my mind," Eve said, her voice tight.

"I'm glad," Patience said softly. "I've been praying all night for your decision—that you'd make the right one for you, and that *Gott* would give me the strength to accept it, whatever it was."

Eve needed strength, too, for that matter, but it was a bit of a comfort to know that Patience had been praying so earnestly.

"I've been so anxious to meet this little boy," Patience said, her gaze moving down to the baby again.

"What will you name him?" Eve asked.

"We haven't settled on a name yet," Patience replied. "We'll probably pick a name from someone in our family—he's our first son, after all." Patience reached out and touched the blanket again. "Do you think I could hold him?"

Eve longed to say no—every instinct inside her wanted to push this woman out of the room and lock the door. But she'd promised them this baby because they were better for him than she was.

"Yah." Eve loosened her grip on the infant, and Patience slid him out of her arms.

Eve's arms felt weak and she simply let them drop, her hands loose in her lap as she watched Patience adjust the baby in her arms. Patience rocked him back and forth and let out a happy sigh.

"I love you," Patience whispered. "You're a beautiful little boy, and I love you…"

Eve felt the tears rising inside her, and she pressed her lips together, trying to stop herself from crying. She couldn't give vent to her grief yet.

"Do you think Thomas could come in now?" Patience asked.

"Yah." Eve nodded. Maybe it would help for her to see the baby with both of his adoptive parents—give her a mental image of how he'd look with his new family.

Patience opened the door and Thomas came inside. He looked hesitantly from Eve toward the baby, but when his gaze landed on the infant, his expression melted and his eyes misted.

"Hey, there," he said gruffly, reaching out to touch the baby's cheek. "Oh… Patience… Wow…"

He didn't seem to have words to pull his emotions together, but Eve could see the way Patience and Thomas looked down at her son, and she knew he'd be safe with them—more than safe. He'd be adored. She was making the right choice… Maybe she'd feel more sure about it later.

"I think you should go," Lovina said. "Don't you, Eve? I think it's time for them to head home."

Eve didn't want them to go, but then, this moment wouldn't get easier for waiting. She didn't trust herself to words, so she just nodded. Patience and Thomas left the room, the baby in their arms, and Eve heard the sound of their steps going down the stairs. There was the murmur of voices and Eve's heart seemed to stretch out of her body, following after them.

She could hear the sound of tack jingling on the horses outside, but she was listening for one last sound from her baby…

The door opened, and then she heard it—his plaintive cry. His wail wound upstairs and sank into her chest like a knife. Then the door shut.

Eve pushed back the blankets and let out a grunt of pain as she dragged herself to the edge of the bed and let her legs drop over the side. Her feet hit the cold floor, and she forced herself to stand, even though her body screamed in protest. With one hand under her stomach, she hobbled across the room to the window, and she sank down against the sill, her arms trembling.

"Samuel…" she whispered. Because being allowed to name him or not, that *was* his name—to her, at least.

She could see the bundle of blankets in Patience's arms, but that was all, and then the horses started forward, the buggy lurching once, then rattling down the snowy drive, taking her baby away.

Eve felt a sob tear through her chest, and she lost her grip on the windowsill, sinking to the cold floor. She wept from such a deep part of her that she thought it might tear her heart right out of her body.

The door opened.

"Eve?" It was Lovina, and then there were hands underneath her, tugging her upward. Eve struggled to rise, and Lovina's strong arms closed around her, and her aunt rocked her back and forth like a baby.

"Oh, Evie…" Lovina crooned. "Oh, Evie…"

There were no words that could explain Eve's grief, and no sympathy that could make it easier to bear. This was a private burden. But all the same, Eve let her aunt help her back into the bed, and when Lovina sat next to her and took her hand, Eve clamped her hand down on her aunt's, refusing to let go.

"You need to eat," Lovina whispered. "Maybe just some tea and sugar? You need your strength, dear. Now it's time to let me take care of you. Please."

Eve didn't answer. Food wasn't going to fix this, because this pain deep in her chest was what it felt like to be a mother without a child in her arms.

Noah worked the shop with Amos that day. It was Christmas Eve, and everyone was picking up last-minute gifts, cheerfully collecting packages as they carried on their way. Outside, the carolers were singing "Jingle Bells," their voices carrying into the showroom where Noah stood, his arms crossed over his chest and his brow furrowed.

They'd finished their orders for the holiday, and they'd all been picked up, except for one. But Noah's mind wasn't on his work. He'd been struggling to keep himself focused all day, but he couldn't seem to do it. Eve was having her baby—or she had it already. How long did these things take? Thomas hadn't come in this morning because they were going to go to the Glick house to wait, and while this wasn't Noah's business, technically, his heart was still lodged in his throat.

A threesome of teenage Amish girls fluttered past the big display window, laughing and carrying boxes from the bakery. He smiled faintly—it wasn't that long ago that he was a teenager, too, and life had been re-markably simple, looking back on it. There was church, and work, and girls that he mooned after…and there had been his mother's visits and his teenage heartbreak over her refusal to stay Amish. His Amish life had given him a structure to grow within. But this Christmas, their Amish life wasn't giving him the comfort he needed.

The bell above the door tinkled, and he looked over to see his mother come inside. She stomped her boots on the mat and looked up with a smile. Her gray hair had some snowflakes clinging to it, and she shook off her coat as she stamped.

"Merry Christmas, Noah," his mother said with a smile.

"Merry Christmas," he said. "Do you have news?"

"It's a boy," Rachel said.

"A boy…" It felt good to know that. "And what about Eve? How is she?"

"Recovering." Rachel's smile slipped. "Giving up her baby is painful for her. But Patience asked her if she was sure, and she was. There was no pressure. But that doesn't necessarily make it easier. So we'll be praying for her as she gets her strength back."

"*Yah*, right." Noah nodded a couple of times. "So the baby…?"

"He's home with Thomas and Patience," Rachel said. "I've come out to buy a few items—more formula, a box of smaller diapers to start off with and one of those little bath seats for newborns—you know?"

"Not really," he admitted with a shake of his head.

"Well, anyway, I'm picking that up for them," Rachel said. "And Rue is just overjoyed to have a baby brother."

"*Yah*, I can only imagine," he said. "So…that's that? She's given up the baby, and everything just…continues?"

"There is tragedy and happiness, all twined up together," Rachel said, and she met his gaze. "Son, are *you* all right?"

"I'm fine, it's just—this is very big," he said.

"The arrival of every baby is a very big event," she replied. "When you were born, everything changed. Your *daet* and I became parents for the very first time. It was like the world tipped upside down for us. That was when your father started talking about this Amish life. He wanted something better for you. I daresay he was right."

"*Yah*…" Noah shrugged uncomfortably. "I'm just worried about Eve."

"She has her aunt with her," Rachel said. "Lovina even closed up the shop today so that she could be there for Eve."

That was something—and he was glad that Eve had someone by her side.

"Would it be…inappropriate for me to go see her?" Noah asked.

His mother's eyebrows went up. "You two have gotten rather close, haven't you?"

Close didn't describe it. What he was feeling for her was a confusing mess, and he knew that there was no future for them, but their friendship wasn't just about Thomas and Patience adopting her baby, or about their hope to help Wollie. Somewhere, he'd slipped past proprieties with her…

"We're friends, I think," he said, but she was so much

more than a friend. Admitting it wasn't going to help, though.

"There are going to be a lot of people visiting Thomas and Patience," Rachel said thoughtfully. "They will be getting a lot of attention and support with their new addition, but there won't be many visiting Eve… I think a visit from her friend would be completely appropriate. And kind."

Noah nodded. "*Yah*. I hoped so. I just wanted to check in on her and see how she is."

"You've grown into a good man, son," Rachel said, putting a hand on his arm. "I'm proud of you."

"Thanks, *Mamm*." He smiled faintly, but he wasn't sure that it helped. Thomas and Patience had just gotten their hearts' desire, and Noah couldn't join them in their joy, because his heart was entangled with Eve.

Amos and Noah closed up early that night—all the shops on Main Street did on Christmas Eve. Before they left, he stopped by the candy shop and bought a little box of chocolates before it closed, too. He couldn't think of anything else that might comfort her right now.

Noah and Amos headed toward home together through the crisp, winter evening, passing by the nativity scene—there were no more bags of donations, since Noah had picked up the last of them that afternoon. But still, the crimson sunset reflecting off the snow and the little nativity stable brought a strange lump to his throat.

"I'm going to drop you off at home," Noah said. "I need to see Eve—make sure she's okay."

"*Yah*, of course." Amos cast him a look. "It's Christmas Eve, you know. They'll be celebrating."

"Will *she*?" Noah asked meaningfully. Somehow,

he doubted that. He'd gotten to know Eve rather well that last little while, and he didn't think she'd be celebrating anything. "Tell *Mammi* I'm sorry. I'll be home when I can."

"I think *Mammi* will understand," Amos said with a nod. "I know I do."

He felt the weight in Amos's words. How much had the older man guessed about Noah's feelings? Amos had been there for Noah through his adolescence, and of anyone, Amos understood him.

When Noah got to their drive, Amos tapped the side of the buggy. "Just let me off here. I'll walk down the drive."

Noah reined in the horses and let Amos off, watching for a moment as he strode through the snow toward the house. *Mammi* would be waiting, and there would be good food and fresh baking... But that wasn't what was calling to Noah right now. Home seemed to be farther away than it ever had before.

He flicked the reins and carried on down the road toward the Glick acreage. He just had to know that she was okay, and then he'd rest a little easier.

Chapter Twelve

Eve sat up in bed, a plate of untouched cookies beside her. And next to that plate of cookies was another plate with a sandwich, and next to that, another plate with a cinnamon bun. Every time someone came up to talk to her, they brought her food, hoping to entice her to eat. She'd had a little bit, because everyone wanted her to eat so badly, but she could hardly bring herself to swallow it.

Her cousins had offered to help her downstairs—they'd set up a little nest for her in the sitting room, they said. But this Christmas, Eve didn't want to be downstairs with her family. She'd only bring them down, if she hadn't already.

She could hear the cousins playing some card games at the table—some subdued laughter, the clink of cutlery on plates. They'd likely be talking about this Christmas for years to come. *"Remember that Christmas when Eve had the baby and it was just so sad?"* But her cousins would be able to file this Christmas away as a somber memory. Eve would be carrying it in her heart for the rest of her life.

There was a tap on her door, and she sighed.

"Come in," she said.

The door opened, and this time it wasn't one of her cousins. Noah filled the doorway, his hat in one hand and concern written all over his features, and she felt a rush of relief to see him.

"Eve?" he said quietly. "Can I come in?"

Eve nodded and gestured to the plates.

"Feel free to eat something," she said.

Noah came into the room, a napkin with another sandwich on top in the other hand. He kept the door open, and he tossed his hat next to the plates, then sank into the chair that had replaced the cradle next to her bed.

"I promised I'd try to get you to eat," he said, handing her the sandwich.

Eve felt her eyes mist. "They're taking good care of me."

"But you aren't eating," he said, his gaze moving toward the untouched plates.

"No…" She'd cried out her tears today—and she felt like she was dried from the inside out, but her grief was still there. And she was sure she'd cry some more tomorrow, and the day after.

"Forget the sandwich," he said, putting it down with the other food, and he pulled a little cardboard box from his pocket. "I brought you truffles."

"Chocolate," she said with a faint smile.

Noah licked his lips and looked down for a moment,

and when he looked up, she could see the deep sympathy in his eyes.

"I had to see how you were," Noah said. "I've been so worried."

"Have you seen the baby?" she asked, looking up at him hopefully.

"Not yet," he admitted. "I had to work at the shop, and instead of going to see him… I came to see you."

He'd come… She hadn't even dared hope that he would. She'd told herself that he'd go straight to his brother's house and everyone would celebrate her child. But he'd come here instead.

Eve's chin trembled. "I did the right thing, giving him up."

He didn't answer.

"Didn't I?" she pressed. "Didn't I do the right thing?"

She wasn't sure what she expected him to say, but it wasn't up to him to be certain. And certainty hadn't come in the last few hours separated from her child.

"My mother came by the shop and told me that they're all really happy and doting on him," Noah said. "If that helps."

Did it? Not really. She'd known they would—her son would be loved dearly, but he wouldn't be raised by the one woman who'd love him more dearly than any other.

"What can I do to help you?" he asked, his voice rough with emotion.

Eve shrugged faintly. "Nothing."

"Tell me there's something," he insisted. "Tell me I can buy you something, dig something up for you. Tell me I can tear something apart!"

"Why?" she whispered.

"Because then I could help! I'm just a man, Eve! I want to fix things—"

Eve put the box of chocolates down on the bed beside her. "It will be easier when I go home."

"When is that?" he asked.

"As soon as I can travel," she said. "Sarah—the midwife—will let me know when I'm healed enough, but she thinks in a few days. There is a certain urgency to be rid of me, I think. She'll let me go faster than she would if I were keeping him."

And then she'd be back with her father, and he'd tell people she had been ill and needed to recover, or something—some forgivable lie so that people wouldn't ask too many questions—and she'd heal. She'd be back in the comfort of her childhood home with the father who loved her just as dearly as she loved her own son.

And she'd have a chance at having that beautiful home of her own.

"How can I reach you?" Noah asked. "Once you've left, I mean."

"You won't." She looked away.

"You don't think you could use a friend?" he asked, but she heard the hopeless note in his voice. "Someone who knows about all of this?"

"You're my child's uncle now," she said, her throat tight. "And I have to let go. I can't stay connected to you—because then I'll always want to know about my baby, and I'll never move on. This is better for all of us."

"I don't think so," he countered.

"Don't you understand how this works?" she demanded. "It's better!"

"It's not better for me!" he insisted.

"Can't you see that I'm doing my best?" she pleaded.

"I'm supposed to just not see you again?" he whispered gruffly. "I'm supposed to pretend that whatever happened this Christmas didn't change anything? Eve, I fell in love with you!"

Eve blinked, and she felt like her heart stopped beating in her chest.

"What?"

"This is terrible, and I know it," he breathed. "This wasn't supposed to happen, and trust me when I tell you, I've been very good at protecting my heart in the past. Just ask the single women in this community. But there's something about you—"

"It's just the pregnancy," she said feebly.

"You're no longer pregnant, and I love you still!" he insisted. "This is not so simple. You're like no one I've ever met. When I'm with you, I feel more alive, and when I'm away from you, I'm thinking about you—"

"What would you have me do, stay?" she asked helplessly.

"What if you did?"

"And your brother?" she asked, shaking her head. "Is he supposed to just hand his son over to you, and let you raise him? You don't see any complications there?"

"I don't know…" He shook his head. "Then I go with you back to your people."

"And never see your family…"

He was silent.

"You know that can't work. We're Amish. Family is what we're all about! Are you supposed to be happy with just me?" She felt hot tears on her cheeks. "I'm not enough—"

"You could be."

"You're only saying that because you don't want to say goodbye," she said. "You know it's true. And I came here to find a family for my baby—I found it. I might hate this. I might never fully heal. But what else is there for me to do?"

Noah reached for her hand and covered it with both of his. "Maybe all I have left is to tell you that I love you."

"I love you, too, Noah…" Her lips trembled. "But that isn't enough to make a family, is it?"

They were Amish, and the right way was very often the hard way. They had accepted that, and they lived according to their principles. She wanted her son to have all the benefits of a happy, thriving Amish family, and he would have that with the Wiebes, but only if she walked away and let him go.

If she stayed, if she loved this man in spite of it all, the happy balance she longed for little Samuel to have would be gone. She'd ruin every chance he'd have…

No, loving Noah wasn't enough.

Noah reached for his hat. He was leaving. What did she expect him to do after a confession like that, after she spurned him? But on Christmas Eve, maybe it was time to tell her whole truth, too.

"I can't be the woman you settled for over one strange, emotional Christmas," she said, her voice shaking. "You want a woman to give you security in a proper Amish life after all you went through with your parents, and I'm just the girl who got pregnant at some Englisher party—"

"Don't say that!" he cut in. "That isn't who you are."

"It's exactly who I am, and it's all I'll ever be in the eyes of the community unless I take this second chance at building a life for myself!" she countered. "So I should take my son back? Anyone who gives up her baby to Thomas and Patience is going to go through this misery, you know. In order for them to grow their family, a woman *has* to lose her child…"

"I know," he said, and his chin trembled.

"If all this is, is pity, some hard feelings because you saw the other side of adoption—"

"It isn't pity, and I do love you, Eve," he said, his voice low and agonized. "But you're right that it's possible to love more than is wise…"

If only a romance between them was a possibility—if all of her heartbreak could be fixed with a simple wedding to a good man. But that only worked if her reputation had been whitewashed, and in Redemption, too many people knew the truth. And it only worked if they could be sure that they'd be happy together five years from now, twenty-five years, fifty-five years… that he wouldn't regret the impulse to marry some pregnant girl and thwart his own brother's deepest wish to grow his family. She'd come here to have her baby and leave. Staying still wasn't an option.

If she could let her child go for his own good, then she could let Noah go, too. Her heart had already been shattered, and it couldn't hold any more grief. If she could keep breathing after giving up her son, she could keep putting one foot in front of the other and take herself out of Redemption and go back home.

"So that's it?" he asked hopelessly.

"I have to trust in the plan I pieced together all those

months when I was able to think straight," she said. "That's what it was for—so that when my heart was in pieces, I wouldn't have to try to think my way through it. I made a plan…"

Noah lifted her fingers to his lips and pressed a warm kiss against her hand. He shut his eyes for a moment, then lowered her hand and released her.

"I'm going to miss you," he said, his voice thick, then he picked up his hat and put it on his head.

She was going to say "Merry Christmas," or even goodbye, but she couldn't force the words out. Noah went to the door and turned back once to look at her.

"I'll be a good uncle," he said, and his voice caught, then he disappeared and his footsteps echoed down the stairs.

That was the last that Eve could take. Fresh tears leaked from beneath her lashes, and her chest ached within as if her heart had truly broken all over again. She bent her head and cried—for her son she'd never raise, for the man she loved but would never marry, for the life she wished she could have with Noah, but couldn't…

Gott's best would have to change along with her circumstances. She couldn't see any other way around it.

Noah's throat felt raw as the frigid winter wind blew snow into his face. The horses clopped peacefully along, but his heart refused to be soothed into the rhythm. He hadn't meant to say all of that to Eve tonight—but now that he had, he couldn't deny the truth. He was in love with her. How had he let this happen? Noah had always been the guy who kept things under control, and falling for the mother of his brother's adopted son—he'd prayed so hard for *Gott* to deliver him from his own emotions. But *Gott* hadn't answered. If anything, his feelings for Eve had only grown after his heartfelt prayers.

His chest felt heavy, his throat tight with emotion. He wanted to cry, but he wouldn't. Not yet. He'd rather skip over this part—the heartbreak, the loss. He'd gone through this when his mother left, and he'd been so certain that he could guard himself against feeling this kind of misery again if he only made the right choices…for all that worked. Falling for Eve hadn't been a choice.

He flicked the reins, and the horses picked up their pace. The wind was brisk, hitting his face and numbing his fingers through his gloves. There were the last of the donations in his wagon—some groceries, more clothes. He'd drop these off with Wollie, and then go home to his family to celebrate Christmas…if he could even manage it.

The moon was high, and the snow glittered in the silvery light. Alone out there on the road with only the horses for company, he lifted his heart to *Gott*.

Maybe it was stupid of me to follow my heart, he prayed. *Maybe I should have found a woman a long time ago and simply chosen to love her. But I don't think love is that simple. Am I wrong? Have I just been stubborn all this time? Because the one time I fall head over boots for a woman, and it's someone so completely wrong for me…*

But he loved her. He loved her so much that even knowing he couldn't be her husband, he wanted to make sure she was okay. He still wanted to find a way to make her pain more bearable. Eve was a woman who'd been through more than most endured in a lifetime, and knowing her heartbreak made celebrating with his brother all that more difficult.

Gott...*let her have the desires of her heart, even though I can't be part of it.*

Christmas had never been an easy time for Noah, not since his *mamm* had left, and this Christmas wasn't going to be any easier.

When Noah turned into Wollie's drive, he could see the electric lights on in the house, and through the curtainless windows, he could see the *kinner* bouncing around in the living room.

Maybe this Christmas wasn't going to be about Noah's hopes, but about Wollie's and Thomas's... Not every man got the desires of his heart, but that didn't mean that *Gott* wasn't pouring out blessings on the community around him.

The front door opened and Wollie came outside, pulling a coat on. He waved to Noah as the buggy came to a stop.

"Merry Christmas!" Wollie called out.

"Merry Christmas." Noah tied off the reins and hopped down, hoping that his own sadness didn't show through, but when Wollie came closer, he hesitated.

"Are you all right?" Wollie asked.

"Yah, yah..."

"No, you're not," Wollie countered.

"Eve had the baby," Noah said. "A boy—healthy and strong. He's home with Thomas and Patience now, so..."

"Yah..." Wollie seemed to immediately sense the complication there. "And Eve is without her child."

"Yah." That was part of it, at least.

Wollie was silent for a moment and he nodded a couple of times. "When Caleb came along, he wasn't… planned. I had a choice to make—marry Natasha, or let her live her life. And I couldn't imagine walking away. But Caleb's arrival changed everything—turned my life upside down in the best and the scariest ways."

"I think babies do that," Noah agreed.

"I daresay this baby turned your life upside down, too," Wollie said quietly.

"No—I mean, my brother is adopting this child, and I'm not the father, and—" Noah sighed. "But *yah*. Babies seem to arrive like a bolt of lightning, don't they?"

Wollie smiled faintly. "I have four, and every single of one them changed me in their own ways."

This baby had changed Noah, too…because of his mother. Eve had been the bolt of lightning into his life, and her child was the one who had pulled them all together. And here Noah was, dropping off donations at a friend's house instead of going to see his brother and meet his new nephew. Because he didn't want to be that baby's uncle—

His heartbeat sped up at the realization, and he sucked in a wavery breath. He wanted to be that baby's *daet*. Not that it mattered what he wanted—he and Eve couldn't work. She was right—they were too different, and they both had plans for how to build a satisfying Amish life for themselves. Falling in love with each other didn't fit in!

"I just came by with a few more donations," Noah said, pushing back his private thoughts. "You know, you're more than welcome to come for Christmas Eve at our place. We'd love to have you."

"Natasha has been making Christmas here, and it's really something…" Wollie looked over his shoulder toward the house. His wife looked out the window and waved, and Noah waved back. Then Wollie turned back. "My parents are coming by this evening, too, so we won't be on our own. But thanks all the same. Maybe we can come see you on Christmas Day, or for Second Christmas."

"*Yah*…that would be good." Noah lowered his voice. "Can I ask you something—man to man?"

"Sure." Wollie stilled, and from inside, Noah could hear the kids' laughter filtering out to them in the snowy cold.

"Do you regret it—marrying an Englisher, I mean?" Noah asked cautiously. "Do you ever wish you'd followed the safe path?"

Wollie was silent for a moment, then he sucked in a breath. "I know this won't make a lot of sense to you, because we were raised to follow the rules and stick to the path. And I know that looking at me right now, you'd think that my life hasn't exactly turned out, but I don't regret it."

"You don't miss the Amish life?" Noah pressed. "You don't wonder if you went against *Gott*'s plan for your life?"

"I do miss it," Wollie said. "And I do want to come back, but marrying Natasha—she wasn't a mistake, Noah. She's…she's everything. She's the one I can turn to, no matter what, and have love and understanding. She's the one I think about when I work long hours, and the one I can't wait to come home to. She's an unexpected gift from *Gott*."

Noah frowned. "I can see how much you love each other, but you can't be Amish with her—"

"Well…" Wollie smiled ruefully. "I can't be Amish with her *yet*, but I'm convinced that *Gott* isn't done with us. Not every path is so direct, but *Gott* is still leading. I know it. I can feel it."

"I admire your faith," Noah said. "Help me unload?"

"Of course."

Noah and Wollie unloaded the last of the donations and carried them into the house. The children were playing in the kitchen with some wooden toys—blocks, carved horses, a little wooden buggy, and some Amish dolls in pink and purple cape dresses. Natasha sat at the kitchen table with a pot of popcorn, and she was stringing it onto some thread.

"Noah's brought over a few more things," Wollie said.

"Thank you so much," Natasha said, standing up. "This means the world to us. I have to admit, we're having a Plain Christmas this year because we don't have any other choice, but I think this is the most grateful we've ever been in our lives."

"We're seeing our grandma and grandpa tonight!" the oldest girl announced. "And we're making popcorn strings to decorate so it will look Christmassy for them."

"That sounds great," Noah said, a smile tugging at his lips. "They'll love that." Then he turned to Wollie. "Come by—anytime. We've got enough to go around, I promise. *Mammi* has outdone herself this year. You know where we're at."

"*Yah*, I know the place," Wollie said. "We'll be driving in the truck—hope that's okay."

"I don't care if you roll over in a snowball," Noah said, winking at the kids who had stopped to look up at him. "Just come."

They said their goodbyes, and Noah headed back out to the buggy. He passed Wollie's parents on his way out, and he waved to them and exchanged a "Merry Christmas."

His heart was heavy, but Wollie's sentiment was rolling over in his mind. *Gott* wasn't finished with them yet... Wollie still had hope that he and his wife could become Amish again together—and that was a phenomenal amount of faith for a man who'd married an Englisher.

And in the sparkling stillness of that Christmas Eve night, he wondered if *Gott* wasn't finished with Noah yet, either...or Eve.

Still, if a man could marry an Englisher and still have faith that *Gott* was working, it gave Noah something to think about. Had he been making wise choices in following a proper path, or was his faith just not big enough for a leap?

Chapter Thirteen

Christmas morning, Lovina came into Eve's room and swished open the curtains. Watery winter sunlight flooded the room, and Eve pushed herself up onto her elbows.

"Merry Christmas, my dear," Lovina said, sitting down next to her on the bed. "I'm sorry to just come barging in here like this, but your *daet* asked me to be the *mamm* you needed, and I'm trying to do that."

"Oh…" Eve said feebly.

"Now, let me help you with your hair," Lovina said, pulling out a comb. "It will feel better once it's combed."

Eve accepted her aunt's solicitous help, and she submitted to her hair being combed. She had to admit that it did feel nice, and her aunt's gentle touch worked through the tangles.

"I noticed that Noah came over on his own yesterday," Lovina said, the even strokes of the comb continuing. "Did he make things harder for you, or—"

"No, Noah didn't…at least not on purpose." Eve's chin trembled. "I don't know if it was just that I was vulnerable and lonesome, or that this situation was so complicated, but we…" Eve wiped an errant tear. "He said he loves me."

Lovina straightened, stopped combing and stared at her. "He said that?"

Eve turned to meet her aunt's gaze. *"Yah."*

"And you said…"

"That I love him, too, but Aunty, it isn't going to work."

"I'm sorry, Evie," her aunt said softly.

"What if I didn't leave my son behind?" Eve asked, and she turned to face her aunt.

"What?" Lovina said.

"What if I took him home with me?" she asked, her voice shaking. "If I keep Samuel, it will break those people's hearts—I know that. And it will make me the cruel and stupid woman who put them all through it, but what if I took him home?"

"What would his life be like, you mean?" Lovina asked softly.

"Yah. With a single mother, and a solid grandfather to raise him… What would that be like?"

"It would be complicated," Lovina said quietly. "People would talk."

"Yah…" She knew that. That was why she'd made her choice to begin with, but she'd thought that after Patience left with her son, it would be easier.

"Evie…" Lovina looked toward the window. "I'm going to tell you something, and your father will be angry with me. I might not even be right to tell you…"

"What?" Eve asked.

"People's opinions mean nothing in the eyes of *Gott*."

Lovina looked over at Eve with a solemn expression. "Nothing."

"It will affect my son all the same," she said.

"Yah…" Lovina sucked in a slow breath. "But life affects us all in some way or other. Your mother died, and that affected you deeply. There was no avoiding that pain."

"True," Eve said uncertainly.

"And I had a similar experience at a party as you did, Eve, except I remembered every second of it, and I didn't end up pregnant…" Lovina licked her lips and looked at Eve sadly.

"Aunty?" Eve whispered.

"I carry it with me still, all these years later. It's affected me, and it's affected how I raise my girls. I'm careful—too careful, some say. But I won't have them assaulted like I was. It affects you whether you want it to or not. I thought that if you couldn't remember it, you might be able to forget…but how foolish was that? And do you know what makes the pain of life harder to bear?"

Eve shook her head.

"Silence." Lovina's chin quivered. "You need to be able to talk about it, and going home to live in that heavy silence while your heart breaks…it *will* affect you. And your son. And your father…"

"What are you saying?" Eve asked.

"I'm saying that life will be hard no matter what. And I truly did think you'd be better off giving this child up and having your chance at a beautiful life. I know what it's like to have your innocence stolen by a wicked boy, and I wanted you to have the chance at marriage and *kinner* that I did. But I'm not so sure that's the right path anymore…unless it's what you want, Eve. I think you need to follow your heart, no matter what other people think!"

Eve's heart hammered in her chest. Life *would* be hard—and there would be talk. Her son would live with stories and stigma…but life would be hard either way, wouldn't it?

And suddenly it all came together inside her, and she knew what she needed to do.

"I can't be happy without my baby… I know I said I'd give him up, and I know I chose the Wiebes to raise him, but I can't do this! I've been in bed all night missing my baby, missing Noah, and my heart is just aching. So it doesn't matter if I could love Noah or not, because I'm about to do something that is going to break his family's hearts. But I'm going after my baby! And I know his family will never forgive me for doing this, but I can't live without my little boy in my arms."

"You're—" Lovina nodded solemnly. "You're taking him back."

"I'm taking him back!" Eve met her aunt's gaze.

"Are you sure about this?" Lovina asked seriously. "You can't just rush in and cause havoc. Are you sure you don't want to think it through? Talk it through? I haven't mixed you up with my own babble just now?"

"I need my baby," Eve pleaded.

"Let's get you dressed, my dear," Lovina said, rising to her feet. "And you can't overdo it, now. You'll have to take it slow. But I will drive you."

Eve had no idea how this would affect the rest of her life, and it may very well be that her son would have been able to avoid the scandal of her name, but asking her to get in a bus and ride away from her infant was like asking her to leave her beating heart behind. She wouldn't survive it.

Would she be able to get married? Maybe not…but life would carry on. She and her baby would still be in *Gott*'s hands, and that was the safest place they could ever be.

If Patience would give him back…

Christmas morning, Noah, Mary, Amos and Rachel gathered in Thomas and Patience's home. Christmas was always a time for family, and Noah listened absently as Amos read the Christmas story in the book of Matthew, Rue locked in with rapt attention. Bible stories were still a novelty for Rue, and every plot twist left her wide-eyed and filled with awe. She'd heard the story of Jesus's birth before—Noah knew that, because he'd been the one to tell her about the wise men—but watching her serious little face soak in the wonder of the real reason for the season made Noah's heart soften just a little bit more.

Gott was real. Jesus was real. And even if his and Eve's hearts broke, there was hope because of their faith. Strange how watching a little girl listen to the story of a stable, some shepherds and a night with no room in the inn could reawaken his own faith.

After the Bible reading, the women set to work whipping up a big breakfast, and the men sat around the table, their chairs pushed out so they could relax. Thomas held the baby, looking down at him with pride glowing in his eyes, and Noah couldn't help but feel a surge of sadness at the sight.

This wasn't just any baby… This was Eve's son.

"Have you decided on a name yet?" Noah asked.

"Not yet," Thomas said. "It'll either be Jacob for Patience's father, or Elmer, for ours."

"I vote for Elmer," Noah said, reaching for the nutcracker and a walnut from the bowl in the center.

"Your vote doesn't count," Amos replied with a laugh. "Amos is a nice name, too, might I add."

This boy would never just be Noah's nephew. Whatever they named him, to Noah, he'd be the son of the woman he'd fallen in love with, and for years, he knew, he'd be looking into this boy's face searching for his mother.

"Do you want to hold him?" Thomas asked.

Noah felt a wave of misgiving, but Thomas handed the baby over, and Noah took a moment to adjust the little guy in his arms. He was so small—no larger than a loaf of bread. The baby pulled his knees up and squirmed until Noah got him settled against his chest. No, this baby would never be just a nephew to him, but the Amish were practiced in sweeping aside uncomfortable feelings. In a community this size, it was either learn to get over it, or have the community disintegrate.

"It still hardly feels real," Thomas said with a shake of his head. "When Rue arrived, it felt very real right away, and somehow with this baby, I still feel like I'm dreaming."

"*Daet*, I can't reach," Rue called, and Thomas headed over to where his daughter was stretching to get a cup above her head, leaving Noah alone with the baby.

The infant opened his mouth in a tiny yawn and Noah touched his cheek with the back of his finger. So small. So soft.

"He's sweet, isn't he?" Rachel asked. His mother came over to where he sat with a dish towel in her hand, and she leaned over his shoulder, looking down at the baby wistfully. Her eyes crinkled when she smiled, and she reached out to touch the baby's toes through the blanket.

"Yah," Noah said. "He's really something."

Rachel tugged a chair up and sank into it, looking at Noah with silent concern.

"I'm fine, *Mamm*," he said.

Rachel pursed her lips. "No, you aren't."

"Mamm—" He didn't want to be cruel, but this wasn't something he cared to discuss right now, with anyone.

"You're still angry with me," she said, tears misting her eyes.

"Mamm, it's not you."

"And that's why you and I have this chasm between us?" she asked, shaking her head. "It's not me? Of course it's me! I left. Isn't that the problem?"

"We don't have to do this now," he said.

"Then when?" she asked. "Son, I love you! And I left this community, and you've never forgiven me for that. But I've forgiven you!"

"For what?" he demanded.

"For not coming with me," she said, and her lips trembled. "I could have forced you to come. You were my children, and I had every right to bring you with me. But I didn't do that—I didn't want to make it into a power struggle. I wanted you to come with me because you loved your *mamm*."

Noah's heart constricted and he blinked back an unexpected mist of tears. "*Mamm*, I loved you—"

"Not enough to come along," she said, then shook her head. "And you blame me for not staying. But love doesn't demand, Noah. Love is patient. Love believes all things and hopes all things, and… I wouldn't force you."

Noah dropped his gaze. He hadn't considered it in quite that way before. She was right—he'd blamed her for leaving, but he'd never stopped to think what it would be like for her having sons who refused to go with her. They'd stood by their faith—and maybe in some ways she'd been equally abandoned.

"Is it my fault that you didn't marry this girl?" she asked softly.

"What?" He looked up at her.

"Oh, you didn't hide it very well," she said gently. "You fell in love with Eve. And she fell in love with you."

"*Mamm*, she's given her son to my brother. There is no way I can marry her."

"Even loving her like you do?" Rachel asked, then sighed. "Son, you like to keep everything in order, lined up, neat and appropriate. You've been like that since you were little. You measure three times and cut once. But with a woman, you can't do that."

Noah adjusted the baby in his arms and patted the little rump gently. "What?"

"I'm serious," Rachel said. "You have to simply let

her…be her! I know you're afraid of everything falling apart on you, so you try to control it and hold it together, but with the most important things in life, we have to let *Gott* hold it together for us. He's the only One who can!"

"I'm not trying to control her," he said with a frown.

"No, you aren't, I agree," she said. "But you're trying to control who you fall in love with, and you're doing your very best to be a good brother. You're trying to control all of the perimeters of your life, and in many ways that's just smart. I raised you to do the right thing, even if it hurts. But sometimes, something hurts because it's *wrong*."

"This is Thomas's son," he said, and his voice caught. "He's not mine…"

"When it comes to your heart, and when it comes to a relationship, even one with your brother, there needs to be some flexibility. If I'd demanded that you come with me to the English world, you would have hated me for different reasons, and we might never have gotten past it."

"You risked losing me completely, though," he countered.

"No, dear," she said with a shake of her head. "I trusted *Gott* to show you your path—and to show me mine. And you know what? *Gott* brought us back together. We were always in His hand. It's not the risk you think when you trust the ones you love to *Gott*."

"Are you suggesting I marry Eve?" he asked. "And be this baby's *daet*?"

"I'm suggesting that you be very certain what *Gott*'s

path is for you, and then you walk that path," she said seriously. "And you let *Gott* take care of the rest."

"What if my brother never speaks to me again?" he asked.

"I have two sons with their hearts entangled in this," she said softly. "And your heart matters just as much as your brother's."

Noah looked at his mother, a new realization flooding through him. Was it possible that *Gott* had brought him a son, instead of Thomas? And if that were the case, could his brother ever forgive him?

"Can you take the baby?" he asked.

The baby let out a little sigh in his sleep, and Noah looked down at him tenderly. This child would always be special to him, and he knew it. But right now his mind was spinning with new possibilities. He needed to get alone... He needed to pray.

"*Yah.*" Rachel accepted the infant from his arms.

"I'm just going to take a walk," he said.

"Of course, son."

Noah bent to kiss his mother's cheek. "Thank you for being my *mamm* and loving me steadily, even when I wouldn't come with you."

Rachel's eyes sparkled with unshed tears, and she nodded. Noah grabbed his coat and plunged his feet into his boots, then headed out into the Christmas cold.

Today was the day they celebrated Jesus's birth— a new chance for the world. And as he strode out through the crunchy snow, he wondered if he'd been going about this all wrong. Did he want to spend the next twenty or thirty years watching this child grow up and remembering the woman he loved?

Or was there a way to follow his heart, after all?

But this was a step he would not take without talking it over with *Gott* first.

Chapter Fourteen

The jostle of the buggy made Eve grimace in pain, but she turned away so that her aunt couldn't see it. She didn't want Lovina to slow down—she wanted to get to the Wiebe house as fast as she could. She needed her son back in her arms where he belonged so that her chest could stop aching with grief.

"Will she give him back?" Dread welled up inside her. What if Patience wouldn't return him? What if she said no?

"We'll go and talk it over," Lovina said. "They're good people. Trust in that."

But trusting in anyone but *Gott* alone was hard to do when her child was in their arms and not hers.

Gott, please give me back my baby! she prayed earnestly. *I was wrong to even try to give him up. Please give him back!*

When Lovina turned into the drive, Eve's heart sped up, and when she reined in the horses, Eve didn't wait for help getting down. She slid to the ground, her boots slipping, and she collapsed to her knees in the crunching snow. Then she pushed herself up, staggering toward the house.

"Eve!" Lovina called. "Wait for me! Eve!"

But she couldn't wait—there wasn't another moment to wait. She needed her baby back, and every breath she took without him felt like it would crush her chest. She made it up the steps and pounded on the door with her gloved fist.

"Let me in!" she cried. "I need my baby! Let me in!"

From inside the house she heard her little Samuel's wail start up. He'd heard her, and she knew that he was responding to his mother's voice. Lovina got to the door and stood next to her, just as it opened and Eve stumbled inside.

The kitchen was warm and smelled of cooking. Thomas stared at her in surprise as she moved past him, scanning the room—everyone was standing now, and every eye was pinned to her. But then she saw her baby, cradled safely in Patience's arms. The other woman stared at her, her mouth open and her cheeks pale.

"I changed my mind," Eve breathed. "I need my baby—"

Patience took a step back, holding the infant closer, but he howled louder.

"Please..." Eve said, tears streaming down her cheeks. "Please, Patience. I know I gave him to you, but I can't give him up. I can't!"

Her knees were shaking, and she felt a strong hand under her arm, guiding her to a chair. It was Amos, and she gratefully sank into it.

"You changed your mind?" Patience whispered, tears leaking down her cheeks.

"I'm sorry." Eve met the other woman's gaze and watched as Patience looked down at the baby in her arms. But he was howling now, arching his little back as he wailed his confusion.

Patience looked over at Thomas and he shook his head sadly.

"She can do that, Patience," he said.

"I know, I just—" Patience's chin trembled. "I fell in love with him..."

This little boy was so loved already, hearts breaking all around him. But Eve couldn't leave Redemption without him. Thomas went to his wife's side and ran a hand over the baby's downy head, then bent down and kissed him.

"He's hers..." Thomas murmured softly. "We have to let go."

Patience crossed the kitchen and gently laid the infant in Eve's arms.

Eve closed her arms around him and her tears flowed. The baby nestled against her neck and settled, pushing his tiny, wet face against her. They were together again.

"Oh, my little one..." Eve crooned. "How I missed you..."

Having him in her arms, she felt like her heart came back together again, closing around him and making her whole once more. She'd carried him these nine months, feeling his movements, getting to know him, and she couldn't stop being his *mamm*, even if it meant she'd never have any more *kinner* of her own. He'd be enough.

"Are you sure?" Thomas asked quietly.

"Yah." Eve nodded. "I can't leave him. I'm sorry—

I tried! I thought if you left with him, it would get easier, but it didn't! And I can't leave him."

"What will you name him?" Patience asked shakily.

"Samuel. He's my little Samuel," Eve said. "He was Samuel since I first saw him, and he can't be anything else."

"Maybe that's why we couldn't find the right name," Thomas said, and his voice caught. "He already had one."

"It's okay," Rachel said, bending down next to Eve. "We understand...don't we?"

Rachel looked up and Patience had leaned into Thomas's arms, her eyes red and her lips quivering. Thomas looked crumpled—but he nodded.

"*Yah*, we understand."

Eve wouldn't stay long. She'd crushed this family— it hadn't been intentional, but she knew she'd hurt them more deeply than anyone would be able to express. It would be their turn to grieve, and she couldn't help them in that process.

Lovina gathered up the baby things that Thomas and Patience gracefully gave her, and Eve went outside into the cold, hugging Samuel a little closer. Her legs still felt weak, but they'd hold her—now that she had her baby back, at least. She looked down at his little face and pressed a kiss against his forehead.

Whatever happened now, she had her son. May *Gott* protect him from the cruelty of gossip...

"Eve?"

She knew Noah's voice immediately, and she looked up to see the big man coming toward her from around the stable. He sped up, his steps plunging deep into the snow as he worked his way through.

"Eve!" When he got to her, he looked down at Samuel in her arms, then into her eyes. "What's happened?"

Would he be angry? she wondered. Would he blame her for the catastrophe she'd caused back there?

"I took him back." Eve licked her lips. "I couldn't leave him, Noah. I know I promised, but I couldn't—"

She expected to see anger, confusion, disappointment even, but Noah didn't even let her stop speaking. Noah leaned down and covered her lips with his, the words evaporating on her tongue. He slipped an arm around her, and the other settled protectively over Samuel's back. When he pulled back, she blinked up at him.

"What just happened?" she whispered.

"I kissed you," he said, his voice low. "Eve, I've been thinking, and I've been praying. I know that your baby belongs with you. I'm certain of it. And I know this seems like an impossible solution, but I want you to stay here with me, and I want us to work this out with my family."

"They aren't going to forgive me," she breathed.

"I think they will," he said. "I've been praying, Eve, and my *mamm* pointed out that sometimes something hurts, not because it's the right thing to do, but because it's wrong! I believe *Gott* brought you to me, not your son to my brother…"

Eve stared up at him. "I had a similar thought…but it was my aunt who pointed it out. Life will be hard whatever we choose, but if *Gott* will bless us—"

"Eve, I love you," Noah said. "When I held your son,

and I looked down at him, I realized I didn't want to be his uncle. I wanted to be his *daet*."

Eve's heard skipped a beat, and she felt like her breath whooshed out of her body.

"Do you mean that?" she breathed.

"I do. I want to marry you. I want to raise him with you. I want to take care of you both."

But things hadn't gotten any simpler—not when it came to his family! She'd just taken her child out of Patience's arms…

"What about your brother, though?" she asked. "And Patience. I promised them a baby, and I took him back! They aren't going to be able to forgive that!"

"Actually—"

Eve startled and looked behind her to see that Thomas and Patience had come outside. It was Thomas who had spoken.

"Forgive us for overhearing. We love that boy, Eve, that's true, but he's *your* son. And we wanted to raise him as our own, but we can love him as our nephew, too. This family is big enough for both of you."

"Yah?" Noah asked in surprise, meeting his brother's gaze. There was a beat of silence between them as the brothers seemed to come to an agreement.

"Yah," Thomas confirmed. "I still believe that *Gott* has *kinner* for our home. My faith is big enough to keep hoping."

"So is mine," Patience said, and she smiled mistily. "He's yours, Eve."

Was Patience referring to little Samuel or to Noah? But when she looked up into Noah's tender gaze, she knew that both were true.

"Will you marry me?" Noah asked quietly.

She nodded, tears welling in her eyes. "*Yah!* I'll marry you!"

"Can we all just come back inside?" Rachel called from the doorway, trying to hold Rue back from plunging out into the snow. "If there's an engagement to celebrate, let's do it as a family in the warmth!"

Eve looked up at Noah, her heart flooding with love. She'd thought that *Gott*'s plans would have changed for her—lessened perhaps—but they hadn't. Here she was with her son in her arms and the man she would marry at her side, and she'd never felt more blessed in her life.

"Merry Christmas," Noah whispered, and he planted a kiss on her head. "Now, you've been through a lot. Let's get you inside next to the stove. You need rest, and food. And no one is going to ask you to put your son down, I promise you that."

Eve smiled up at him and she brushed a tear from her cheek. "I love you."

"I love you, too."

This was the Christmas that *Gott* gave Eve His very best, and her heart's desire, in the form of a little baby snuggled in her arms—and the man who'd be his *daet*.

Epilogue

In the new year, when the sun shone bright on new fallen snow, Eve stood in the bedroom where she'd delivered her son in her aunt's house. This room was steeped in memory for her, but today she was here getting ready to take her vows.

Eve had always wanted a proper wedding—big and joyous, with celery soup to feed a county. But somehow, after Noah had proposed on Christmas Day, she didn't care so much about the size of the wedding. It seemed more important to be able to settle into a home with Noah as his wife—to start her life as a wife and a mother.

So instead of waiting until the fall, they decided to get married at the end of January in her aunt's living room with extended family only as their guests, and Bishop Glick to perform the ceremony. Eve's *daet* and siblings came out for the wedding, her baby no longer a secret, as they came together as a family to celebrate Eve's new marriage and her precious little boy. Secrets, after all, had a poison to them, and they'd all agreed that while they could be discreet, they'd always be honest.

Upstairs in the bedroom, Eve adjusted her *kapp* once more in the mirror, then looked over at her father, who sat in a chair with his grandson up on his shoulder, gently rubbing the baby's back.

"You make a beautiful bride, Eve," her *daet* said with a fond smile.

"Yah?" She blushed. "Thank you, *Daet*."

"I'm sorry I tried to make you—" Her father's voice choked. "I'm sorry that I—"

"It's okay, *Daet*," she said. "I suppose we all thought that *Gott*'s best for me would change."

"You're a good woman, Eve," her father said. "And you've got the kind of faith that Samuel will tell his *kinner* about."

Eve went to her father's side and bent down and placed a gentle kiss on Samuel's plump cheek. He was growing fast, a strong, sturdy baby with rolls and dimples in all the proper places. When Eve's mother had told her that she'd done her best, Eve hadn't understood it then. But she felt like she did now, now that she was a mother, too. What else could a wife and mother do but her best? Perhaps those simple words, "I did my best," were a quiet, Amish victory as a woman crossed the threshold into glory.

She'd done her best. She'd given her all. She'd loved with everything she had.

Eve would follow her *mamm*'s example and do the same—she couldn't help it! Noah and Samuel filled up every corner of her heart, and if one day she could tell her *kinner* that she'd done her best, she'd feel like she'd succeeded in walking the path *Gott* had so graciously given her.

She'd be honest. She'd be faithful. She'd love them with everything she had.

Samuel woke up with a squirm and a cry, and Eve eased him out of his grandfather's arms. She snuggled him close, and her son blinked up at her with those dark, round eyes. Perhaps he'd be awake for the ceremony, after all. She'd have to see if he consented to being cuddled by someone other than his mother for the next hour or two.

"Let's go down," her father said with a smile. "Your fiancé is waiting."

And at the thought of Noah downstairs with their mingled families, Eve's heart skipped a beat. She was about to promise this man the rest of her life…and she couldn't wait for it to begin.

* * * * *

If you enjoyed this story, be sure to pick up the first book in Patricia Johns's Redemption's Amish Legacies series,
The Nanny's Amish Family

Available now from Love Inspired.

And look for more Amish romances from Love Inspired, such as An Amish Winter, *coming January 2021!*

Dear Reader,

Have you ever wondered if it's possible to ruin God's plans for your life? We mess up, we disappoint ourselves and those around us, and it certainly throws a wrench into our own plans…but does it surprise God? I don't think it does. In fact, I don't think we're strong enough to mess up God's plans for us.

That was the thought I had when I began writing this story. God starts with our rock bottom, and He can give us the beautiful life He's planned for us all along.

I hope you enjoy Eve and Noah's story of redemption and second chances. And I hope you never give up on your own life's story, either!

If you'd like to follow me, you can find me on Facebook, Twitter, or my website, at patriciajohnsromance.com. I'd love to connect with you!

Patricia

**WE HOPE YOU ENJOYED
THIS BOOK FROM**

LOVE INSPIRED

INSPIRATIONAL ROMANCE

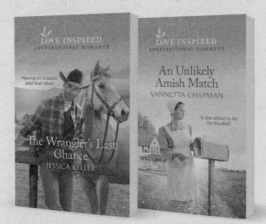

Uplifting stories of faith, forgiveness and hope.

Fall in love with stories where faith helps
guide you through life's challenges, and discover
the promise of a new beginning.

6 NEW BOOKS AVAILABLE EVERY MONTH!

LIHALO2020

AN AMISH WINTER
by Vannetta Chapman and Carrie Lighte

Amish hearts are drawn together in these two sweet winter novellas, where an Amish bachelor rescues a widowed single mother stranded in a snowstorm, and an Amish spinster determined never to marry falls for her friend's brother-in-law when her trip south for the winter is delayed.

THE AMISH BAKER'S RIVAL
by Marie E. Bast

Sparks fly when an *Englischer* opens a store across from Mary Brenneman's bakery. With sales declining, she decides to join a baking contest to drum up business. But she doesn't expect Noah Miller to be her biggest rival— and her greatest joy.

OPENING HER HEART
Rocky Mountain Family • by Deb Kastner

Opening a bed-and-breakfast is Avery Winslow's dream, but she's not the only one eyeing her ideal location. Jake Cutter is determined to buy the land and build a high-end resort. Can his little girl and a sweet service dog convince him and Avery that building a family is more important?

THE RANCHER'S FAMILY SECRET
The Ranchers of Gabriel Bend • by Myra Johnson

Risking his family's disapproval because of a long-standing feud, Spencer Navarro is determined to help his neighbor, Lindsey McClement, when she returns home to save her family ranch. But as they work together, can they keep their forbidden friendship from turning into something more?

A FUTURE FOR HIS TWINS
Widow's Peak Creek • by Susanne Dietze

Tomás Santos and Faith Latham both want to buy the same building in town, and neither is willing to give up the fight. But Tomás's six-year-old twins have plans to bring them together. After all, they want a mom...and they think Faith is the perfect fit!

AN UNEXPECTED ARRANGEMENT
by Heidi McCahan

Jack Tomlinson has every intention of leaving his hometown behind—until twin babies are left on his doorstep. He needs help, and the best nanny he knows is Laramie Chambers. But proving he's not just her best friend's irresponsible brother might be a bigger challenge than suddenly becoming a dad...

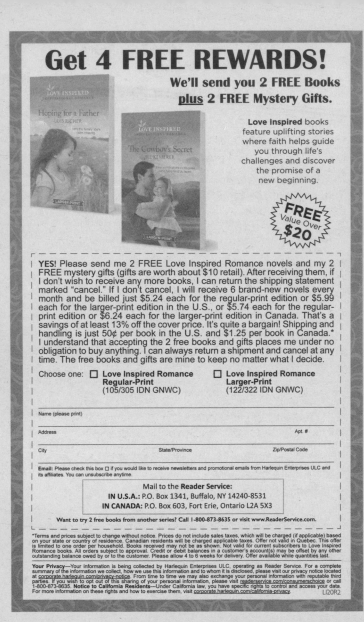

*When a city slicker wants the same piece of land
as a small-town girl, will sparks fly between them?*

Read on for a sneak preview of
Opening Her Heart
by Deb Kastner.

What on earth?

Suddenly, a shiny red Mustang came around the curve
of the driveway at a speed far too fast for the dirt road,
and when the vehicle slammed to a stop, it nearly hit the
side of Avery's SUV.

Who drove that way, especially on unpaved mountain
roads?

The man unfolded himself from the driver's seat and
stood to his full over-six-foot height, let out a whoop of
pure pleasure and waved his black cowboy hat in the air
before combing his fingers through his thick dark hair
and settling the hat on his head.

Avery had never seen him before in her life.

It wasn't so much that they didn't have strangers
occasionally visiting Whispering Pines. Avery's own
family brought in customers from all over Colorado who
wanted the full Christmas tree–cutting experience.

So, yes, there were often strangers in town.

But this man?

He was as out of place as a blue spruce in an orange grove. And he was on land she intended to purchase—before anyone else was supposed to know about it.

Yes, he sported a cowboy hat and boots similar to those that the men around the Pines wore, but his whole getup probably cost more than Avery made in a year, and his new boots gleamed from a fresh polish.

Avery fought to withhold a grin, thinking about how quickly those shiny boots would lose their luster with all the dirt he'd raised with his foolish driving.

Served him right.

Just what was this stranger doing *here*?

"And didn't you say the cabin wasn't listed yet?" Avery said quietly. "What does this guy think he's doing here?"

"I have no idea how—" Lisa whispered back.

"Good afternoon, ladies," said the man as he tipped his hat, accompanied by a sparkle in his deep blue eyes and a grin Avery could only categorize as charismatic. He could easily have starred in a toothpaste commercial.

She had a bad feeling about this.

As the man approached, the puppy at Avery's heels started barking and straining against his lead—something he'd been in training not to do. Was he trying to protect her, to tell her this man was bad news?

Don't miss
Opening Her Heart *by Deb Kastner,*
available January 2021 wherever
Love Inspired books and ebooks are sold.

LoveInspired.com

LOVE INSPIRED
INSPIRATIONAL ROMANCE

IS LOOKING FOR NEW AUTHORS!

Do you have an idea for an inspirational
contemporary romance book?

Do you enjoy writing faith-based romances about small-town
men and women who overcome challenges and fall in love?

We're looking for new authors for Love Inspired,
and we want to see your story!

Check out our writing guidelines and
submit your Love Inspired manuscript at
Harlequin.com/Submit

CONNECT WITH US AT:
www.LoveInspired.com

Facebook.com/LoveInspiredBooks

Twitter.com/LoveInspiredBks

Facebook.com/groups/HarlequinConnection

LIAUTHORSBPA0820R

LOVE INSPIRED

INSPIRATIONAL ROMANCE

UPLIFTING STORIES OF FAITH, FORGIVENESS AND HOPE.

Join our social communities to connect with other readers who share your love!

Sign up for the Love Inspired newsletter at **LoveInspired.com** to be the first to find out about upcoming titles, special promotions and exclusive content.

CONNECT WITH US AT:

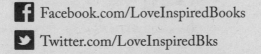

Facebook.com/LoveInspiredBooks

Twitter.com/LoveInspiredBks

Facebook.com/groups/HarlequinConnection